Cutting it Close: Racing for Redemption

Riley Scammahorn

CONTENTS

CHAPTER ONE

TREPIDATION

THURSDAY, MARCH 23, 2028

"There are days where I miss racing. I miss feeling all the power from the engine vibrate through my soul and how the car would force me deeper into my seat when I downshifted. When the whole world went past me in a blur as all my problems, fears, and sorrows drifted away."

It had been over twenty years since Derek Stetson retired from his racing career. Since then, he settled down with his beautiful wife, Shannon, and their daughter, Autumn. Though racing and cars have never left his heart and mind, Derek lived a quiet life. He worked from eight to five at his local mechanic shop, making barely enough to cover the bills. Afterward, he came home to his wife, who always took an interest in his work endeavors, and his daughter, who was always excited to see him.

Derek was an averagely tall person who was starting to add some grey hair to his brown, buzzed hair and mustache collection. Due to growing up in east Texas but always moving around for races, he has a slight southern accent that most people don't even notice. He always wore black or grey cargo pants with his button-up mechanic's shirt at work. When out and about, he stuck to the same routine of wearing dark-shaded blue jeans with a t-shirt and, as his name implies, a black Stetson hat.

After work, Derek was more worn out than usual. Fortunately, the day was over. So he could relax and cruise home to his loving family in his 1966 Plymouth Valiant sedan. Derek loved his car because it wasn't ludicrously fast, and it wasn't hard to fix either. Instead, it was simple, relaxing, and peaceful. The 225 Slant-six under the hood wasn't obnoxiously loud, but it made enough noise to make Derek happy when he put the pedal down.

While driving, he noticed a billboard advertising the annual televised racing event, "The Behemoth Grand Prix." Of course, he didn't think much of it. However, it did cause Derek to reminisce about his racing days for the rest of his drive home.

Pulling into the driveway, Derek could see the house lights on and the shadows of his five-year-old daughter jumping around the entryway. Seeing his girls every day after work always brought him joy. But, tonight, Derek didn't even get both feet inside the house before Autumn jumped and tackled her father to the ground.

"Hi, daddy!" she exclaimed.

"Hi honey," Derek responded, "Can't you let me get inside now and again before you tackle me? Then we could land on some nice soft carpet for once."

"But daddy! I can't wait that long!"

"You tacklin' your daddy again, young lady?" Shannon smirked.

"Nooo," Autumn claimed with the most innocent of expressions.

Autumn took her father's hand, "helped" him up from the ground, and led him inside, where Shannon awaited them.

"How was work, my love?" asked Shannon.

"Tiring per usual. Lots of nuts, bolts, tires, and oil." Derek responded in exhaustion.

Derek got lost in his wife's beautiful bronze eyes. She was a couple of inches shorter than himself, with brunette hair and natural red highlights. She spoke with a slightly thicker Southern accent, making his heart melt every time. Well, almost every time.

"I know this ain't what you want to hear right now, but we just got another bill in the mail."

"I'll take care of it," sighed Derek.

"Not before you give me a kiss, old man!" Shannon proclaimed as she grabbed his shirt and yanked him close. "There, now you can go adult."

Derek sat down at his desk and started up his computer. Before paying the bills he could barely afford, he checked his email. At the top of his inbox was an email in big, bold letters that read, "BE OUR GUEST OF HONOR." Confused, Derek opened the email to discover it was an invitation to race in the Behemoth Grand Prix as their guest of honor. Digging deeper into the invitation, he found dates, times, and a phone number to call to RSVP his position with the tournament organizer. Derek was in disbelief; he ignored the email and went about his evening.

The three Stetsons were enjoying their meal at the dinner table that night. The table conversations were reasonably typical. Did anything special happen at work today? How was school? The usual small talk one would hear. Then, Derek mentioned the racing email. Shannon was speechless.

"Well? How'd you respond!?" She insisted.

Derek, looking confused, replied, "What do you think I did? I ignored it. I can't race competitively anymore."

"So, you're not even considering it?"

"How can I? You know just as well why I can't race anymore."

"I know, my love. I'm sorry. I know how much you miss racing. I can see it every time you get in the car. It pains me to see you so down."

At this point, little Autumn interrupted, "Dad's going to a race?"

Derek sighed and explained to her why it was a bad idea for him to race again. Autumn understood and cleared her place at the table. After dinner, they all got ready for bed, for Autumn had school, and Derek and Shannon had to work the next day. In bed, Derek and Shannon shared a kiss and wished each other a good night. Unfortunately for Derek, the conversation at dinner time triggered a recurring nightmare.

It was back when Derek Stetson was a professional touring car racer in the US Touring Car Championship. Even though he had won many races, he never achieved first place in the championship as a whole. Derek sought to change that. He was pursuing a first-place title in the final race when suddenly, the left front tire on his 2016-spec Corvette C7.R exploded. The Corvette lurched into the infield, caught air, and rolled to the guard rail, where the car instantly went from a hundred miles per hour to zero. Fortunately for Derek, the vehicle did not catch fire. However, the paramedics quickly discovered he was paralyzed from the waist down. The ambulance rushed him to the nearest hospital, where the doctor realized it was only temporary paralysis caused by shock and nothing was broken. When Derek regained consciousness, the doctor explained how he would regain full use of his legs if he followed a vigorous physical therapy program. However, the doctor also warned that if Derek was to get into another similar accident, the paralysis could be permanent due to the previous injury. Thus, ending Derek's racing career.

Derek shot out of bed. Drenched in sweat, his breathing became rapid, and his heart rate quickened. Shannon woke up and immediately knew what had happened. She held Derek in a firm hug and began reassuring him that it was just a dream and that he was okay. They worked together to slow down his breathing, eventually calming him down.

"You had the dream again, didn't you?" Shannon asked calmly.

Derek nodded as he began to cry into her shoulder. They sat there for a while to let Derek get through his anguish. Then, Shannon grabbed a towel from the bathroom and dried the sweat off him. Once they diffused the situation, they snuggled against each other and returned to sleep.

CHAPTER TWO

SUBDUING FEARS

SATURDAY, MARCH 25, 2028

D erek was in his garage the following weekend, working on his pride and joy. A 1969 Dodge Charger Daytona. It was a dark, metallic, royal purple with a carbon fiber wing, which was the Daytona's signature feature.

He had replaced the pop-up headlights with flush-mounted ones for easier maintenance and a sleeker look, and he replaced the stock rims with some black-painted American Racing ones. Derek had heavily modified his Daytona to match and surpass the performance of his old race car: Roll Cage, semi-slick tires, racing suspension, and drivetrain, and a brake system that was so powerful, the whole car could stop on a dime. It was powered by a 6.2-liter supercharged Hemi, which with heavy modification, produced 921 horsepower and 798 foot-pounds of torque, which powered a 7-speed manual transmission. This machine was pristine, inside and out.

"I figured I'd find you in here!" Shannon shouted to get Derek's attention.

Derek slid out from under the car and hugged his wife. They went to the far side of the garage, where they each grabbed a glass of iced tea and sat on a car's rear bench seat that was fashioned into a couch.

"You want to race again, don't you," Shannon said calmly.

"I'd be lying if I said no," Derek replied, slumping his head in disappointment.

"It's okay, my love. We just have to figure some stuff out, that's all."

"You aren't opposed?"

"I'm not inherently for it, but I'm also against you feeling that you can never live out your dreams again. I feel like that would be rather cruel."

They both went back and forth, trying to figure out what to do. On the one hand, Derek racing again would be foolish because of his higher risk of injury. Not to mention that with him being 42 years old, his reflexes aren't what they used to be. But, on the other hand, racing would fill a hole in Derek's soul that has been missing for a long time. Finally, Derek and Shannon agreed that the strongest argument is that the million-dollar prize for winning this tournament would fix their financial situation. However, even with all of the pros and cons laid out, one obstacle was still in their way, Derek himself. It's no doubt that Derek was particularly terrified of racing again. After much thought, the two partners couldn't determine which emotion would win, passion or fear.

"I really want to do this, but I couldn't live with myself if I became permanently crippled and unable to support my family. I barely feel like I'm able to support my family at all, even right now." Derek revealed on the verge of tears.

"Hey, that's not fair to yourself. You work hard to support this family and do a damn fine job too. It's not your fault that your medical bills drained us and the cost of living is increasing." Shannon rebutted. "Maybe this race is what you need to overcome your fear. Don't you remember when I got caught in the riptide at the beach a long time ago?" Derek nodded. "Well, it was years before I even contemplated going back into the ocean. Do you remember how I got through that? You were there."

Derek sighed, "Autumn and I practically forced you in. We helped you relearn the joy of swimming and that you'd be okay."

"I think Autumn definitely did the heavy lifting for you, old man." Shannon laughed and socked Derek on the shoulder. "Well, does that answer our question?"

Derek couldn't believe his ears, "Yes. I will race. And I promise I will do my best to win and get us out of debt."

"Do you want to tell your daughter, or shall I?" Shannon smirked.

Both parents went inside and told Autumn the news. At first, she was confused and concerned. She didn't want her dad to get hurt. Then, Derek explained to her that he needed to overcome his fear. Autumn skeptically accepted that answer. However, her mood changed substantially when they told her she could watch him race on TV.

Derek stood from where he was sitting. "Well then, it's settled. I guess I have a call to make."

The line didn't ring for long. Then, a cheerful, upbeat woman answered the phone.

"This is tournament organizer Nora Barnes; how may I help you?"

"Hello, my name is Derek Stets-"

"Derek Stetson!?" Ms. Barnes interrupted.

"Yes, ma'am. That's me."

"I was getting worried you didn't get my email. Welcome to the show!"

"Uhm, thank you, ma'am. I don't quite understand what's going on."

"No problem, let me explain everything...."

Nora proceeded to fill in Derek about the tournament. It's an annual, pay-per-view televised series located in a different state each year; this year is Derek's home state of Texas. These races have no separate race divisions, which was particularly interesting to Derek.

"No divisions? What on God's green earth does that mean?" Derek questioned.

"Oh, Mr. Stetson, that's what makes our show so interesting! As long as your vehicle passes our rigorous safety inspection and is deemed competent enough to keep up, you can take any type of car you'd like."

Confused, Derek questioned, "ANY car?"

"Yes, Mr. Stetson. ANY CAR. There was one year when we had the top-of-the-line Italian supercars all lined up, ready to race. You want to know who won?" Ms. Barnes asked excitedly.

"What won that year?"

"A heavily modified 1960 Volkswagen Beetle."

Derek was in shock. A beetle! Against Ferraris, Lamborghinis, and whatever else originates there nowadays. Unfortunately, that didn't exactly ease any of Derek's concerns. This meant he'd have to supply his car and pit it against engineered masterworks and, even scarier still, other people's built-up project cars. Ms. Barnes continued to elaborate that the tournament consisted of three races.

The first race is a circuit race on the roads of whatever state they're in that year, just like the Long Beach Grand Prix in California. It's a three-lap race where the top twelve racers advance to the next round, and the bottom twelve are eliminated.

The second race is the only one run on an actual racetrack, the longest race of the three, spanning 100 miles. The show sponsors provide a pit crew, gas, and extra tires for this race. This race is a test of endurance, build quality, and speed, where only the top five drivers will advance to the finale.

The third race is arguably the most intense of the three. Like the first race, it uses public roads that have been closed off. Tensions are exceptionally high in this race because it's the deciding factor. Who's going to win the grand prize of one million dollars? Who will claim one of the most prestigious racing titles in America? And most importantly, who's going to be invited next year? Of the five drivers in the finale, only the podium winners are invited to next year's event.

"Do you have any questions, Mr. Stetson?"

Derek stared at his monitor blankly while processing all the information he had just received. "Ma'am... I have more than several questions."

"How about this, Mr. Stetson? Why don't you drop by our headquarters tomorrow so I can answer all of your questions in person?"

"That's an excellent idea, Ms. Barnes; I will enjoy meeting you in person tomorrow!"

Derek hung up the phone and walked over to his bed, where Shannon was reading her book.

Shannon peeked over the pages of her book, "Good call?"

Derek face-planted into the bed. "Woman! What have you gotten me into?"

Shannon did everything in her power not to laugh. She failed hysterically.

CHAPTER THREE

ACQUIRING ANSWERS

SUNDAY, MARCH 26, 2028

D erek arrives at the address provided to him. The building is at least ten stories tall and occupies about a suburban block's space. On the top of the entryway, in big, bold letters, read Behemoth Parts.

As he stepped out of the revolving doors, he heard a familiar and excited voice, "Mr. Stetson!?"

"Ms. Barnes, I take it?" Derek chuckled.

She was an average-sized African-American woman with short, wavy black hair and brown eyes. Most people assume she's in her early to mid-thirties, but they get shocked when they discover she's in her early fifties.

"Let's chat in my office," Ms. Barnes continued, waving her hand directionally.

Derek followed, taking in the magnificence of the building he was in. The whole building was monochromatic and extremely clean. The floors were polished like mirrors, and there wasn't a speck of dust on any surface.

"Welcome to Behemoth Parts, Mr. Stetson. Allow me to showcase what we do here. As you could've guessed, we are a parts company, but we are different. We are different because we sell *everything*: Engine, transmission, suspension, electric, interior, body panels, the works. And we don't just sell the new stuff. No, no. We try to produce and sell every automotive year in history. Whether you're looking for an OEM or aftermarket part, we got the right part for customers. If we don't? We'll work with them directly to manufacture the parts they need."

"Very impressive," Derek proclaimed, clapping, "I use your services often. My car back home is at least fifty percent Behemoth parts."

"Your Daytona, right?" Ms. Barnes returned.

Derek was stunned. It made sense why she had access to his vehicle information, but he didn't expect her to look him up.

"Ya. My Daytona. Can you explain to me what's going on?"

"Gladly," Ms. Barnes said as she sat down, "We have become quite the prestigious event to win over the years. So we had to find a fair way to allow people of all kinds a shot at the title. Because let's face it, if we just upped our admission cost, you'd only get the super snobby rich folks with their European supercars; as fun as that might be for some, that's not why we created this tournament. So, we kept the admission fee very low at $200. With that said, we have an extensive screening process. We are looking for genuinely good people and drivers and must keep it diverse for the audience, cars, and people alike. So we now have big trucks, supercars, muscle cars, minivans, and everything under the sun.

"I understand." While scratching his stubbled chin, Derek proclaimed, "So where do I fit into all this? I never applied, nor did anyone screen me or my car."

"You, Mr. Stetson, are our guest of honor. We always have scouts on the lookout for unique vehicles that could race in our event. I believe your car was discovered by one of our scouts in California when you attended the Grand National Roadster Show a couple years back. We then wrote down all of our potential candidates, including you, and randomly picked one from a jar. That is how we select our guests of honor."

Derek was shocked, "So you mean to tell me that I got selected at *random* to race in one of, if not *THE most prestigious races* in the US?"

"Yes, sir. And a good thing, too, we don't have a muscle car in the running yet this year."

Concerned, Derek asked, "I'm the *only* muscle car there?"

"Yes, Mr. Stetson. As I mentioned earlier, anything goes. Our only major guideline for racing is that you cannot use experimental fuel or NOS."

"Are there any other rules I should know about Ms. Barnes?"

"Yes. While contact is inevitable in racing, you will be immediately disqualified if blatantly done on purpose.

The last important one we strictly enforce is that no professionally ranked racers are allowed."

Now Derek was even more confused. "You realize I used to be professionally ranked, right?"

Nora laughed hysterically. "Yes, sir. I am well aware of your past. However, since your retirement, you haven't been on those leaderboards, have you?"

Derek chuckled along with Nora at the remark.

Ms. Barnes walked Derek out of the building.

Nora stopped at the door to say goodbye. "I have one last question for you, Mr. Stetson." Derek turned around to listen, "Are you ready for some redemption?"

Puzzled, Derek replied, "Redemption, Ma'am?"

"You heard me right. Redemption. Let's just say that I've been in your shoes, Mr. Stetson. I know what it's like to chase after a dream only to fall short. You inevitably lose hope."

That struck a nerve with Derek. He could never describe his emotions towards racing after retirement, yet a woman he had just met knew it immediately.

"Well, ma'am. That's a question I never knew to ask. And I'll tell you what... I'm happy you did because *redemption* is what I've been searching for."

CHAPTER FOUR

BOOKS BY THEIR COVERS

THURSDAY, JUNE 29, 2028

Race day was forty-eight hours away, and the crowd at the scene was beyond anything Derek had ever seen. Everywhere he looked, there was another car to look at. It was the largest, most spectacular car event he'd ever attended. The diversity was immense as well. To Derek's left were hundreds of Ferraris, Lamborghinis, Porsches, Mercedes, Aston Martins, and some cars he didn't even recognize. To his right was filled with every Japanese import you could imagine: Skylines, Supras, Rx-7s, Lexuses, all heavily modified. To his astoundment, there was a whole section dedicated to pickup trucks. Everything was there, from a tiny Nissan Frontier to a gargantuan trophy truck with tires larger than some cars. This place had it all: hot rods, custom cars, rally, drift cars, and everything in between.

"I do believe I am in heaven!" Derek chuckled while he pinched himself to make sure he wasn't dreaming.

Because of his affinity for muscle cars, that's naturally where Derek checked out first. He saw a Ford station wagon with a supercharged engine so large he wondered how anyone could drive it; you couldn't see anything! Many cars Derek saw from the fifties and sixties were kept all original by their owners. Derek was impressed with these because it is hard to keep anything original. But, what intrigued Derek even more, were the resto-modded muscle cars like his Daytona. Cars that looked like old vehicles from the past, yet packed all of today's new technology. Even a couple of electric conversions of old cars have surprised Derek. At the end of the line of muscle cars stood a 1956 Ford F-100 pickup truck. You could see every layer of paint peeling off and exposed, rusted steel showing everywhere.

Derek approached the owner of the truck, who was sitting in a lawn chair beside it. "This your truck, sir?"

The man turned towards Derek, "Why yessir! This here is my pride and joy."

"What's her story?" Derek asked, wondering why this older man would let his 'pride and joy' get in such an awful condition.

"Well son, I'd love to tell ya! This here is Annie. I found her out in a barn about 40 years ago and I have restored her to her best self."

"I'm sorry sir, I don't mean to be rude, but she doesn't exactly look like her best self."

"HA! Don't let ol' Annie fool ya. She may be showing her age on the outside with her patina, but allow me to show you her heart and soul."

The old man lifted up the hood of his truck.

Derek's Jaw dropped, "Is that what I think it is!?"

"Yessir! That there is a genuine Ford 427 Big Block motor. That beaut' there won the 1966 Le Mans race over in France!"

"I stand corrected sir. You have built a damn fine machine."

"See son, don't be so quick to judge them books by their covers. Besides, if you really want to reduce weight, rust will always be lighter than carbon fiber!" The old man cackled in laughter.

Derek continued to drool over all the different cars when the live band suddenly ended their song on the main stage. The crowd roared. Then, a familiar voice rang over the speakers.

"Ladies and gentlemen! Welcome to the Behemoth Grand Prix!" yelled Ms. Nora Barnes over the cheering party. "Do we have a special event for y'all. Our first race will consist of three laps around a closed course in the rolling hills of central Texas!" Another pause was taken to allow the thunderous applause to die down. "While our drivers make their way towards the stage for their introductions-"

Derek immediately darted towards the stage.

"-allow me to introduce to you our podium finishers from last year's Behemoth event from the beautiful forests of Oregon!" Ms. Barnes exclaimed to get the crowd even rowdier than they already were. "Last year, this brave young woman battled the pack in her home state in order to place in third. In her infamous 2013 Lamborghini Veneno, Sandra Dorette!"

Derek was struggling to weave his way through the dense crowd.

"Up next, this young man has been battling for the title for five whole years now but has always found himself to be the runner-up. Will that change this year? Only time will tell. From Los Angeles, California, in his 2018 Ferrari FXX-K Evo, Killian Briggs!"

Derek could finally see where he was supposed to be. He saw the stage entrance.

"And finally! The winner of last year's Behemoth Grand Prix. Hailing from the one and only Detroit Michigan. In his 2016 Ford Racing GT Le Mans, Warren Stonewood!"

The crowd roared their highest when that man walked out on stage. It startled Derek as he was panting up the steps backstage. At this point, Derek had no idea who was announced because he was focused on getting to the stage. But, alas, he made it to where he needed to be, and he could now catch his breath.

Derek was the next person to be announced to the immense crowd. Even in his prime racing career, he had never stood in front of that many people. But, unfortunately, he didn't have time to stress over it because he heard Ms. Barnes proceed.

"For this year's guest of honor, we have a very special driver with us. Racing in his home state of Texas, in his 1969 Dodge Charger Daytona, Derek Stetson!"

Derek stepped on stage to shake Ms. Barnes's hand. To Derek's surprise, the crowd was reasonably responsive when his name was called. He was a nobody from the middle of nowhere. Yet people cheered for him as if they had known him for years. Derek thought of the old man with the rusty truck.

"I guess my cover ain't so bad after all," Derek said under his breath.

After waving to the people, he left the stage.

CHAPTER FIVE

INSPECTION

THURSDAY, JUNE 29, 2028

S weat was beading from Derek's forehead. His pride and joy had never been through a proper racing inspection before.

"What did I forget?" Derek thought as he stared into the inspection garage with deep concern.

The first thing the 4 inspectors looked at was the suspension. On the lift, they raised the Purple Daytona over their heads. Every inspector had a bright flashlight so they could get a better look.

Derek saw one jot down some notes on his clipboard.

They checked the brakes next. The rotors spun as the inspectors checked the pads.

Derek noticed another one taking notes. He tapped his feet anxiously.

The tires were placed back on, torqued down, and the car was lowered back onto the ground. Half the inspectors popped the hood and checked the engine compartment, while the other half inspected the interior.

Derek noticed them nod, approving his roll cage and seatbelts, which provided some relief. But, unfortunately, Derek could not see what was being checked in the engine bay. After some time passed, they took the Daytona out of the garage to inspect the next car.

"Mr. Stetson?" someone asked.

Derek turned around to discover the inquirer, "That's me."

"Ah, Mr. Stetson. I'm Mr. Sullivan, the racer coordinator. I do exactly as the name implies. I have your inspection results. The head inspector actually wanted me to give you his praises. He said that 'It is one of, if not the, best car he's ever looked at,'" he proclaimed.

Derek was shocked, "Well, thank you both!"

"No problem, sir," Mr. Sullivan politely said, "Here is your report, sir."

Derek pondered over the report. Just as Mr. Sullivan told him, his Daytona passed with flying colors. At the bottom of the page was a competitiveness score.

"Excuse me, Mr. Sullivan? What is this competitiveness score?" Derek asked.

Mr. Sullivan looked up from his clipboard, "Oh, we've made a range from one to ten to rate how competitive your car will be compared to the other racers; one being your car will be passed by a snail and ten being faster than wildfire. Everything will be left in your smoke."

Derek chuckled, "So I guess my eight is pretty good then!"

Mr. Sullivan's head shot back toward Derek's report, "What? Let me see that!" He took it from Derek's hands and darted off toward the inspectors. Derek could see the funny expressions of shock Mr. Sullivan was articulating to the inspector. Then, suddenly, Mr. Sullivan walked back to Derek.

"I understand it a bit better now. So, the amount of horsepower you're producing certainly helped your score but wasn't the deciding factor," explained Mr. Sullivan, "We get cars here with thousand-plus horsepower all of the time. You barely even passed that hurdle. What sets *you* apart is your suspension setup. According to the inspectors, provided you drive it correctly, this thing will be just as competitive in the corners as the straights."

Derek was shocked, "A muscle car like mine doing well in corners against everything else out there!?"

Mr. Sullivan nodded in agreement, "I was just as surprised as you. I've never seen a muscle car rank so high."

Mr. Sullivan handed Derek a form, "Here's how our tournament point system works …."

- First – 20 Points

- Second – 18 Points

- Third – 15 Points

- Fourth – 12 Points

- Fifth – 10 Points

- Sixth – 8 Points

- Seventh – 5 Points

- Eighth – 4 Points

- Ninth – 3 Points

- Tenth – 2 Points

- Eleventh – 1 Points

- Twelfth – No Points

"Seems pretty straightforward," Derek noted while shrugging his shoulders.

"Excellent! Let's get you to your garage."

They both walked across the compound to a large aircraft hangar. In the hangar were twenty-four bays with a twin post lift, a massive, fully stocked toolbox, and all the necessary equipment to work on their vehicles.

"Here is where everyone will be working on their cars for the race," Mr. Sullivan explained, "Everyone has the same equipment, so there's no need to *borrow* anyone's tools and such. There's no strict rule about staying in your own bay because we aren't a prison here." Mr. Sullivan laughed at his own "joke."

Derek wasn't laughing, "Is there any measure in place to prevent sabotage?"

"Ah, yes," cameras are set up all around us to prevent cheating. We are very diligent about that."

Derek caught a glimpse of his car from the corner of his eye.

"Whelp, here's your garage space. After your races, re-placement parts are on the house, provided you can provide us with the broken part as proof; other maintenance and or modification parts are heavily discounted. All tires and fuel are provided by us to prevent cheating. I will leave you to explore your new home away from home." Mr. Sullivan explained, then turned away.

"*EXCUSE ME!?*"

Derek looked up from his new toolbox. It appeared his neighbors were arguing about something. Intrigued, he silently walked to the other bay to investigate further.

He saw a man and a woman arguing over what looked like a heavily modified Mazda Mx-5 Miata. Judging by their argument, it was safe to assume that the Miata belonged to the woman.

"You heard me! Your car came from a cereal box. It was probably some stale, off-brand one, too!" yelled the male racer.

Without missing a beat, the woman responded, "HA! This is coming from 'Daddy's *Money*' over there. I hate to break it to you, but at least my car isn't STOCK!"

"Oh shit," Derek mumbled under his breath.

The guy lightly pushed the woman, which pissed off Derek. As the woman drew her arm back to return a blow, Derek shouted, "BREAK IT UP!" as he rushed to separate them.

CHAPTER SIX

FEUDS, FRIENDSHIPS, AND FAMILY

THURSDAY, JUNE 29, 2028

Derek stood between the two racers. Keeping them off each other was more challenging than he anticipated. The woman especially.

She yelled, "Killian, I'm going to...."

"Hey! Knock it off. Both of you!" Derek shouted as he pushed them both away. "Leave the debate for the track. Then you can actually prove your point rather than make empty threats."

"Oh, my threats ain't empty." The woman spat at Killian.

Dodging her spit, Killian returned, "Whatever! You two don't scare me!"

"Then why are you trying to fight us then?" Derek countered.

Apparently, his statement didn't merit a response from Killian because he walked away without saying a word.

"My name is Carmen by the way. Carmen Winters," she said.

Carmen was about an inch or two shorter than Derek, was in her mid-thirties, and had crimson red hair and blue eyes. She said she was from Arizona and a single mother to her fifteen-year-old son, Cole Winters. She was in shape and naturally very stoic, but she seemed to loosen up once she let someone in.

"Nice to meet you, Carmen. What the heck was all that about?" Derek questioned.

She tensed, "That prick over there is Killian Briggs. The most snobby, Italian, money for brains son of a...."

"Okay there, I get your point." Derek interrupted.

"What?" Carmen sarcastically rebutted, "I was going to say 'son of a wonderful person.' You should really have more faith in me, cowboy."

"Mmhmm. Sure you were." In a desperate attempt to change the subject, Derek pointed to her car, "Is this beaut' yours?"

Carmen smiled, "Yessir! This beaut' is mine," she mockingly said, using a fake southern accent.

She was the proud owner of a 1994 Mazda Mx-5 Miata. The paint was dark, *blood* red, with black Work rims. Derek swears she color-matched the red on the car to her hair. It had a widebody kit on it with a large spoiler equipped.

"Why on god's green Earth do you have such obnoxiously large downforce equipment on a Miata?" Derek questioned.

Carmen burst into laughter. After snorting several times, she answered, "Because you haven't seen the powerplant yet!"

Her 2,201-pound Miata was powered by a 2.6 liter, four-rotor, R26B racing engine. Mazda used the same engine in the 787B Prototype race car in 1991. With some modifications, Carmen's Miata produced 718 horsepower and 466-foot pounds of torque.

"Woah," exclaimed Derek, "with a car so light, how do you manage to find any grip?"

"Between the amazing tires provided to us by Behemoth, an all-wheel drive system, and a 10-speed sequential gearbox."

Derek's jaw dropped. "Ten gears?!"

Carmen shrugged, "I'm still working out the kinks. He eats through those gears like I starve him."

"Nothing a little trial and error tuning can't fix," Derek suggested reassuringly.

Autumn didn't let the phone ring for more than a second, "Autumn here, can I take a message?"

"Well Ms. Stetson, that depends... Do you want to talk to your dad or not?" Derek said as he tried to keep a straight face.

Autumn yelled, "DADDY!" so loud that Derek had to pull his phone away from his ear.

"How's my big girl doing?" asked Derek.

"Dad, you'll be so proud of me! I went into the house garage and I put my car on the ramps and mommy helped me fix the battery!" Autumn shouted, unable to contain her excitement.

Derek's heart melted, "I am so proud of you my Autumn-leaf! When you're old enough, you can help me more often in the big garage with real cars. How does that sound?"

"Does that mean I can work on your racecar with you?" Autumn chuckled with glee.

"That could be arranged. I think I hear my spark plugs about to die on me, maybe you could help me with those when I get back."

Autumn gasped, "NO! Daddy, you have to replace those right this instant before your race! Your engine could explode!"

"My engine is not going to explode silly," Derek laughed, "I'll change them first thing in the morning before qualifying okay?"

"You better," Autumn threatened.

Derek was taken aback, "You better watch your tone missy, or I might have to tell your mother not to give you dessert."

"Sorry daddy," she was quick to reply.

"That's alright love. Can you please hand the phone to your mom please?"

"Hello?"

"Hey darlin'," Derek replied with a big grin.

It's as if Shannon knew because she also had a huge smile, "How did everything go today?"

Derek proceeded to spill the dirt on the day's events. First, he mentioned the insane number of cars and the old pickup with the big engine. Then, he told her about the crowd's thunderous applause when he walked on stage. Despite Derek's nervousness, she was happy to learn how the Daytona did in the inspection and exclaimed at how Carmen and Killian were roasting each other.

When Derek mentioned how he intervened and stopped a physical fight from starting, Shannon groaned, "Always gotta be the hero don't ya?"

"What?" Derek questioned, surprised, "I don't want to be a hero."

Shannon gave an obnoxiously loud "HA," and explained, "You may not want to be the hero honey, but you always find a way to become one. Just ask your daughter."

The conversation continued for some time; they didn't even realize how late it was. They finally agreed that Derek needed much-needed rest for his big day tomorrow. But before they could say goodnight, Derek voiced his concerns...

"What if I crash again?"

"Derek Stetson!" Shannon strictly yelled, "You get your head out of that zone right now, ya hear!?"

Derek realized the severity of the situation. Shannon only goes drill sergeant mode if it's a big deal. "I know honey, you're right. I'm sorry."

"Damn right," Shannon threatened.

"Well, now I see where Autumn gets her sassy tone," Derek chuckled.

Shannon turned bright pink, "Oh, shut up!"

"So you're teaching her 'shut up' now?" Derek outright burst into tears laughing.

"You know what? You need your sleep! I know you will be amazing tomorrow darlin'. You got this. You know your car better than you know yourself. Trust it. Feel it. And know that your girls are rooting for you back home."

Chapter Seven

Qualifying

Friday, June 30, 2028

Derek was on edge. He hadn't raced in years and wasn't as confident as his wife thought. "It's time to face your fears, Stetson, not succumb to them," Derek ordered as he took a deep breath. Fortunately for Derek, he had time to get a rhythm before the race during practice and qualifying.

It was explained to Derek that today was the only time during the tournament that requires a qualifying round because your placement in each race afterward is determined by the position you finish in the race prior.

Due to his last name starting with "S," he had to wait a while for his turn to take his practice laps. Fortunately, this allowed

Derek to view the other racers' practice. He was glad he did. Several racers had gone out to drive already, and more than half spun off somewhere on the course. Derek needed a plan because he was discovering how difficult this race would be.

Then it hit him....

Derek ran to find the nearest map of the road course. Once he saw it, he traced the route on a blank paper. His plan was formulated.

Derek started muttering the plan to himself under his breath, "Alright, Derek. What you need to do is take the first practice lap at slow speeds..." meaning seventy to a hundred miles per hour, "Then, you take each lap a bit faster. On the qualifying lap itself, put no more than fifty percent. This will keep the car in good shape for the race itself. I bet half of these guys have to replace something major before the race."

"*DEREK STETSON TO THE START LINE PLEASE! Derek Stetson to the start line please.*" Blared the loudspeaker.

"I guess that's my cue," Derek smirked to himself.

Derek gripped the wheel. He pulled his visor down on his helmet, and with the clutch in, he revved his engine to signal he was ready. The world around him went quiet; the distractions and fears disappeared. The light turned yellow, and Derek had a split second before releasing the clutch and launching his Daytona into the practice lap. By the time the clutch was out and the car started going, the light was green.

The purple Daytona launched forward. Derek got up to speed in no time, but he limited himself and stuck to his plan. Derek studied every corner, bank, and straightaway while staying within a hundred miles per hour. Derek cruised around these country roads at this speed, knowing he'd be going more than twice as fast during the real deal. The car purred through the straights, hairpins, and chicanes. Driving has always been therapeutic to Derek, but this was something else; he was practically in heaven.

Rounding the last corner, Derek sped up for laps two and three. He needed to understand this course at speed while also keeping his racing ability under wraps. Derek knew that the other racers were gauging him as an opponent, and he also knew that if he went slow enough, they would underestimate him. That's precisely what he wanted.

Back at the shop, every racer was busy repairing and tuning their cars for the big qualifying lap later that day. As Derek suspected, many of them had tremendous damage to be fixed. He saw one poor guy have to replace an axle. Not exactly what you want to be worrying about hours before the qualifiers.

On the other hand, Derek only needed to check the basics: oil, brakes, tires, other miscellaneous fluids, and other minor maintenance. Because of his expertise, Derek finished up in no time at all.

Once he deemed the Daytona ready, Derek sat down at his workbench and took notes on the map he had drawn earlier. On every corner of the race, Derek marked the direction of the turn (left/right) and what gear he needed to be in to safely make it through the corner. That's when he really discovered how challenging this race would be.

Half of the thirteen-mile track consisted of high-speed sections where Derek was confident the competition would easily break two hundred miles per hour. The other half of the course was extraordinarily technical; there were sharp, ninety-degree corners, hairpins, chicanes, elevation changes, banked and flat corners, and sections where you had to drop into second gear from fourth or fifth. It was a masterpiece of a road course, and Derek was excited to be a part of it.

The moment of truth. Derek's qualifying lap. He gripped the steering wheel in anticipation as he stared down the red light in front of him.

"You know what to do Derek," he instructed himself, "limit yourself to sixth gear, don't get ahead of yourself, be patient, and keep it clean."

The tree dropped a red light. Derek revved his engine mildly in preparation. Then, it went yellow. He dropped the clutch and accelerated as fast as the car would let him. Green.

The Daytona was eating gears like it was on its last meal. Derek had to suppress it. He shifted early on purpose to hide the actual performance of the car. The first chicane approached; Derek quickly downshifted to fourth and went straight through it. Heading downhill, Derek saw the second sharpest corner. But he prepared for this; before he met the turn, he softly pressed the brakes and shifted down to second, allowing the engine to do all the heavy braking for him.

"Good job Derek!" he exclaimed after executing a clean racing line.

Derek effortlessly weaved through the country roads at over a hundred miles per hour. The next challenge approached; the double hairpins. Derek slowed down and shifted into third. He rounded the one-eighty corner at eighty miles per hour and accelerated as hard as he could until he had to slow down to third again to make the second opposing hairpin.

"Okay, Derek, that didn't suck, but we need to make up some time."

His foot slammed against the floor, and the monster under his hood roared! Derek hit one-hundred-seventy miles per hour in sixth gear as he ripped through the corner. After weaving through more corners, Derek caught the most challenging corner here. It consisted of a ninety-degree corner located on a minuscule backroad intersection. Derek had to apply the brakes more aggressively this time as he downshifted to second gear. He dropped seventy miles an hour in a matter of seconds. Fortunately, a surprisingly quick section through a small suburb came after this dangerous turn, where most people spun out.

While going one hundred thirty miles per hour, Derek noticed a speed limit sign, "Oh shit. I did not just see a twenty-five speed limit sign. That's crazy! I wonder how much that ticket would cost me?"

Derek's thoughts were interrupted by the third most dangerous and misleading corner. It looks like a nice, effortless, fast corner at face value. But once you're on top of it, you realize how sharp it is. Derek lost count of how many people spun out into this poor lady's side yard during practice. He slammed the brakes and downshifted his way into third gear.

Once he made the corner, Derek sighed in relief, "Okay, all three of the hard parts are done. Let's open her up and keep going!"

The last half of the race was filled with shallow, fast corners that the Daytona's suspension demolished painlessly. Taking corners over one hundred fifty miles per hour as if it were a Sunday drive to church. He finally saw the finish line. Derek ignored his sixth gear rule and shifted into seventh, breaking two hundred miles per hour on the home stretch. Unfortunately, he had to brake before the finish line for the corner that immediately followed it to avoid crashing, thus slowing his time further.

Derek felt confident in his lap time even though he didn't know what it was yet. Finally, he accomplished his goal of having a clean qualifying lap. Now all Derek had to do was wait for the results.

Twiddling his thumbs back at the garage, Derek awaited the results like everyone else. Suddenly, a black Toyota pickup rolled into the center of the hangar. All twenty-four racers approached the vehicle until they practically surrounded it. Out came Mr. Sullivan with a sheet of paper. He climbed into the bed of the truck to make his announcement.

"Ladies and Gentlemen! Thank you all for an amazing qualifying day. As you all know, tomorrow's race will decide which half of you all get to continue racing. With that being said, you know how important today was. Let's hear the results."

Derek didn't pay much attention to who was placed where. However, he was very annoyed that Killian qualified for the pole position. Someone driving a Mclaren Senna placed second, and the defending champion Warren placed third with his Ford GT. Names kept getting called out, and people celebrated in their own ways, and even more, people were visibly nervous; the farther back you are tomorrow, the harder you had to work to place first. Derek, on the other hand, remained calm. Finally, his name was called, and he qualified 17th. Now all that was left to do was win the real thing tomorrow.

Chapter Eight

Breaking Through

Saturday, July 1, 2028

The crowds were immense. The cars and trucks were ready, and so was Derek. Derek was confident in his ability to win on this course. He memorized every corner, every gear change, and every straightaway. *I'm ready*, he kept repeating to himself. Then his eyes widened... a massive truck pulled up right behind him! Derek frantically turned around to get a better look. Sure enough, there was a 2011 Ford F-150 Raptor behind him. It was clearly lifted, and God only knows what kind of power that thing was producing.

Derek took a huge gulp, "Why is there a lifted truck in a road race? Those two usually don't go together. Talk about *anything goes*."

Amidst his bewildering thoughts, Derek heard the loudspeaker, "DRIVERS! Start, your, engines!"

The ground violently shook as all 24 vehicles' engines started up, and Derek's HEMI roared to life. Derek shut his visor and gripped his steering wheel. As much as he wanted to just floor it on yellow, he didn't know the speed of all the cars around him. Going too fast would lead to Derek rear-ending the 2001 Nissan Skyline in front of him. Then again, he didn't want to get rear-ended by the truck, either.

The tree turned red. Every racer was revving their engines in anticipation. Derek saw the glass on a nearby building flex and warp from all the vibrations. Finally, the tree started counting down. Red, red, yellow... green.

Derek released the clutch and floored it. The cars around him, doing the same, launched out of the starting grid. Several vehicles didn't have enough traction off the line because Derek saw multiple cars burning rubber. Derek kept pace with the vehicles in front and behind him; they were all within inches of one another. The driver of the Nissan in front of Derek took the first chicanes too wide, allowing Derek to come up the inside and pass him without looking back.

The first sharp left approached, and Derek was one of the only few racers who managed to perform it clean. Derek chuckled because he had a plan. Not only did he study the course itself, but he also studied his opponents on it. As the second gear left corner approached, Derek immediately pulled right onto the shoulder of the road and came to an almost complete stop. As he idled along the shoulder, he saw precisely what he expected. All of these drivers around him didn't know when to brake. As a result, several cars braked too late, causing them to understeer and go straight out of the corner. Derek counted maybe ten cars going directly through the turn or getting crashed into by the people who couldn't stop in time. Then, he saw a window of opportunity between the wreckage to bolt out of the corner and continue the race.

With that maneuver, Derek managed to launch himself to thirteenth place. He kept pushing his Daytona to catch up with the next racers. They all shifted back and forth between fifth, fourth, and third gear, trying to make their cars as fast as possible. Then, they approached the double hairpins. Derek was quick to gauge his opponents in front of him. Both the Porsche and BMW were rear-wheel-driven cars, and they both were pushing their limits, trying to keep up with one another. The first hairpin approached, and both competitors entered the corner too fast, causing them to oversteer and slide wide of the ideal racing line. Derek took advantage of their mistake and passed them both on the inside.

"Keep fighting amongst yourselves, ladies! I'm just going to squeeze by y'all real quick." Derek shouted at the two rivals, who clearly couldn't hear him.

Approaching a fast corner, Derek noticed something in his peripheral vision. The Ford pickup truck was off-road, cutting the corner!

"That lousy cheater," Derek grumbled to himself as he chased after tenth place.

Unfortunately, the Pickup's sneaky trick pushed Derek back into twelfth. Derek knew getting around him would be an unusual challenge because his truck was so big it nearly took up the entire road, especially when drifting in a corner. But, bobbing and weaving through the course, Derek finally understood why someone would bring a lifted truck to a race like this. There was one thing the Ford didn't count on, though... the next second-gear right turn.

The truck swung left to give him the best line through the corner, leaving Derek with the inside. Derek wasn't thrilled with the line he had to take, but he knew it would be worth it because, right as he predicted, the pickup truck had to brake early to safely make the turn. Since Derek had a better-equipped vehicle for road racing, he could launch past him and brake closer to the corner than the truck.

Shifting into second, Derek launched himself out of the corner and onto the chicane, where he'd find ninth, tenth, and eleventh-place racers. They all passed the chicane without missing a beat, but Derek knew what to do when they got to the deceptive third gear left. The Audi in ninth place did, too, because he took the corner beautifully as the Porsche and the Subaru lost grip and swung wide. Derek attempted to pass them both but was quickly denied when the Subaru promptly regained control and cut him off.

Fortunately for Derek, the technical half of the lap was done, and now he could unleash all one-thousand-fifty horsepower at his disposal. Derek shifted into fifth gear and got to work. He passed the Subaru and the Porsche with ease. He could hear them trying to speed up behind him, but his car was just too quick for them. The Daytona made short work of catching up to the Audi from before. Derek took the outside line placing him bumper to bumper with the Audi. The driver beside him knew he was there and had to out-brake him in the next left corner. To the shock of the

Audi driver, Derek hit the brakes first! The Audi driver brakes shortly after Derek, but to his surprise, Derek swings around behind him for the better line and is already in front of him.

"Ha-ha! Oldest trick in the book, my friend!" Derek shouted again, knowing the racer he just passed couldn't hear him.

The final stretch of the road was by far the fastest, which allowed Derek to catch up to the rest of the pack. Again, he put the gas pedal to the floor. Only shifting to sixth, not his top gear, Derek reached two hundred miles an hour. The second Derek attained this speed, he slammed on the brakes and shifted his way down to fourth to safely make the next corner.

Derek's speed paid off because he caught up to the leading pack. The top eight racers were all in one group, fighting for positions. Derek was right behind the eighth-place Koenigsegg. They were fender to fender when they crossed the line, marking lap two.

CHAPTER NINE

REVELATIONS

SATURDAY, JULY 1, 2028

Derek felt alive. The vibration from the Daytona's HEMI coursed through him as he traveled over a hundred sixty miles per hour next to some of the fastest machines ever built; by people much more intelligent than he is. With his confidence rising further, Derek slingshotted past the Koenigsegg 1:1 and managed to squeeze in the gap between the Mercedes AMG and the Audi R8. In the mirror, Derek saw visual frustration in the drivers he had just passed.

"Didn't think I'd be passing you today? Think again ladies and gents'!" Derek exclaimed to himself.

Approaching the sharp left corner, Derek hit the brakes and started downshifting towards second. After completing the corner, Derek was astounded and saw Carmen's Miata. He could hear her car eat through five or six gears before Derek could shift into fourth.

"What the...!" Derek shouted as his jaw dropped to the floor pan.

The Miata disappeared from Derek's vision as they approached the double hairpins. Derek was caught behind an Aston Martin DB9 and a McLaren Senna. Both drivers knew what they were doing because they were battling for position amongst themselves and successfully defending the entire road. The three cars entered the second hairpin, and Derek still could not find a window.

Suddenly, the DB9's brakes locked! Derek, already slowing down for the corner, swerved out of the way of the Aston Martin. Glancing back, he realized that the driver of the DB9 hit the brakes too late and too hard, causing him to slide off the track. This left the battle for fourth up to Derek and the McLaren Senna. Derek knew that he'd have to make his move quickly because there was no way he could surpass the Senna's performance in the corners. With its massive wing and aerodynamic body style, that car produced a car's worth of weight in downforce to keep it planted on the road. Navigating the small neighborhood again, Derek saw Carmen's Miata struggling and sliding through the technical corners, leaving a wide opening for the McLaren and Derek to pass her.

Derek was millimeters away from the McLaren's rear bumper. Approaching a small straight-away, the Daytona and the Senna caught up to the leaders. Warren was defending first place against Killian until disaster fell. Coming to the tight chicanes, Warren's Ford GT didn't have enough room to make the corner safely with Killian's Ferrari in the way.

Warren spun out! The Ferrari and the McLaren slammed on their brakes to keep themselves from crashing with him, but not Derek. He saw a window of opportunity that he was willing to risk. Instead of slamming on the brakes like his competitors, Derek downshifted into fourth and launched toward the minuscule gap. Before Derek could fully comprehend the situation, he was in the lead.

"YES! Let's GO Derek!" he screamed in excitement.

Now he could fully unleash the beast inside his car. In the fast half of the race, Derek pushed his Daytona harder than he's ever made any car before, including his race-spec Corvette from back in the day. He didn't brake as hard for the corners and had the gas pedal to the floor whenever he could get away with it. The Daytona power slid through the corners as Derek kept the hammer down. Passing two hundred miles per hour often, Derek was in heaven. All of his troubles and fears faded away. The world passing him by left him more relaxed than ever. Even at such grand speeds, Derek's heart wasn't racing; it was slow, consistent, and calm.

Unfortunately, Derek's euphoria was interrupted by a sharp, fourth-gear left corner. Derek slammed on the brakes, knowing fully that he was too late to engage them. He rushed his car through the gears and downshifted from seventh to fourth. All four wheels locked into place as Derek skidded towards the turn. He let off the brakes to allow them to unlock and regain enough traction to make the corner.

Aggravated, Derek shouted at himself, "Damn it Derek! Focus!"

Fortunately for Derek, he had made a large gap between the rest of the pack and himself, so his disastrous mistake didn't cost him any positions. But his sense of euphoria turned into a hurricane of anxiety. His mind raced faster than his heart, and he gripped the steering wheel as if his life depended on it. He recalled his accident and how it destroyed him physically and emotionally. The fear of crashing again practically paralyzed him as he slowed down for another turn.

"What are you doing, Derek!?" he interrogated, "Why are you risking your life this way? You can't do that to your girl's man! That's not fair to them!" Derek was on the brink of tears. "Damn it, what are you doing, Derek!" he yelled as his breath became irregular.

Derek knew that if he wanted to finish safely and stay in the lead, he needed to calm down. So as he passed the line again, marking the third lap, he forced himself to take a deep, square breath. Repeating the exercise resulted in his breath normalizing and his heart regulating.

After calming down, Derek took in his surroundings. He knew it was the last lap and had a commanding lead, but he just had to keep it.

CHAPTER TEN

MISCALCULATIONS

SATURDAY, JULY 1, 2028

D erek's rearview mirrors were vacant. Still pushing at a hundred-ten percent, he wanted it to stay that way. But, unbeknownst to Derek, his car was feeling the pressure. He started taking corners a gear higher than he initially planned due to his newly acquired confidence. Still, as Derek approached the double hairpin corners for the final time, it all became abundantly clear.

Shifting his way down to third gear, Derek compressed the brake pedal. The car wasn't slowing down quite as efficiently as it used to. Unfazed, Derek took the corner fast with a squeal of his tires. As the second hairpin approached, Derek pressed the brakes and turned in earlier with little repercussions other than more tire squeal. Derek realized what was happening as he floored out of the last U-turn. His tires were going bald, causing him to lose massive quantities of much-needed grip. He approached the sixth-gear left turn only to discover that his Daytona wasn't turning! He eased off the gas to give his tires some extra grip for the corner; he still slid straight for the edge of the road. Tapping the brakes, he led his car toward what should have been a fifth-gear right turn. Derek soon discovered that this corner, once taken in fifth gear, could only be completed in fourth.

Derek could not find the grip to turn, and he still had more than half of the lap to go! He slammed on the brakes and shifted his way down to second as he approached the neighborhood. As soon as Derek completed the corner at his slowest pace yet, the rest of the pack caught back up. Derek did everything in his power to protect his position. But as he and Killian's Ferrari approached the last corner of the neighborhood, Killian and three other racers effortlessly overtook Derek.

"Damn it!" Derek shouted, "What the hell am I supposed to do now!?"

Trying to keep pace, Derek put the pedal to the floor. He was successful in keeping up until another corner approached.

Then, knowing it was necessary to stay on the track, Derek slammed the brakes again and shifted to third gear, where the Daytona used to be in fourth. Before he knew it, the leading pack of four escaped his view, and the next group of four was on his tail. Derek recognized them too. Warren, Carmen, and the two racers in the Mercedes AMG and the Audi R8 tried to get a better line through the chicanes. Then, knowing he had to do something to keep them all at bay, Derek ripped the e-brake, making the Daytona's rear-end slide out. He blocked Warren in his Ford GT, taking up the entire road width. Understandably, cautious since the last time he was in this stretch of road, Warren backed off from Derek's maneuvers.

On the other hand, Carmen saw a window of opportunity when Derek started to straighten out and simultaneously passed Warren and Derek. Realizing his mistake, Derek attempted to straighten out his car for the approaching left turn and regain some lost momentum. Unfortunately, the three cars behind him took advantage of Derek's opportunity and passed him without breaking a sweat.

Derek furiously realized that he was now in only ninth place. He would be disqualified and go home empty-handed if he lost more than three more places. He did not want to come home a failure again.

"If I take it slow and preserve my tires, I will certainly get passed by enough people to disqualify me. But if I push it and risk popping my tires completely off, I'm disqualified anyway for not finishing the race," Derek muttered to himself, "Unfortunately, it's a lose, lose situation. Screw it. Let's go."

So he kept his foot down and kept pushing forward. The Daytona was sliding in every corner because Derek was trying to keep up with his old pace with bad tires. He could see the tire smoke in his mirrors. As he came out of a slow corner, more than smoke appeared in those mirrors. Before Derek could leave the corner, the Aston Martin DB9 and a Nissan R34 Skyline overtook him, leaving Derek in eleventh. Even though his situation was dire, there was still hope, for Derek could see the final corners before the starting grid. He was nearly there!

Derek's hope was short-lived because the Ford Raptor appeared from the shadows. Blatantly disregarding any rules of the road, the truck cut through the last two corners of the track as if it were a straight line. Derek swore at the pickup and slammed his fist into the dashboard. Furious, he chased down the truck in the final straight and crossed the finish line in twelfth place.

Coming to a stop, Derek rested his head in his crossed arms on the steering wheel and whispered to himself, "What the ...."

CHAPTER ELEVEN

"CALM" INVESTIGATIONS

SUNDAY, JULY 2, 2028

I t took Derek the rest of yesterday to cool off; he was pissed and confused. But he knew that if he had searched for answers and confrontations yesterday, he would have created more harm than good. So after sleeping it off and refreshing himself over a nice cup of hot coffee and a steak and egg breakfast, he searched for answers from Mr. Sullivan. Fortunately for Derek, Mr. Sullivan is a very easy person to find.

"Hey, Sullivan!" Derek shouted sternly. "I have several questions for you."

Mr. Sullivan, startled by Derek's directness, turned around and headed towards him and asked, "How may I help you, Mr. Stetson?" as calmly as possible.

"Hi. First of all... *What the hell*!?" Derek shouted, forgetting that he was supposed to be calm, "Why on God's green Earth were my tires the only ones wearing prematurely, and since when is blatantly cheating by cutting corners allowed in racing, because that pickup truck yesterday was out of line. And…"

"Woah, woah, woah, Mr. Stetson. Calm down! Let's clear some things up, shall we?" Mr. Sullivan interjected.

Derek apologized, "Sorry, sir. I didn't mean to yell. You must understand how frustrated I am about yesterday's race."

"It's quite alright, Derek," Mr. Sullivan returned while sighing, "Why didn't you come to me yesterday with these complaints?"

Derek chuckled, "Because I probably would've kept yelling, and I sure as hell wouldn't have apologized."

"Well, thank God for that. I had enough angered racers at my throat yesterday as it was. It's hard to tell people with no skill that they lost because they have no skill." Mr. Sullivan snickered. "Anyway, let's figure out what happened to your tires, shall we? That definitely confused a lot of people yesterday. I happen to know that a lot of people thought you had it in the bag!"

"Trust me, sir, I thought I was one of them too."

Derek and Mr. Sullivan walked over to the Daytona to inspect the tires. When they arrived, Mr. Sullivan was in shock.

"Excuse me, what the heck is this!?" he said, pointing at the tires.

Derek shrugged his shoulders, "Behemoth tires?"

"Well, yes, that is true, but someone gave you the wrong tire tread!"

Confused, Derek pondered, "Aren't these semi-slick tires, though? That's what racers should be using on country roads, right?"

Clearly angered, Mr. Sullivan marched to Carmen's Miata to compare the tires, "Ah-ha! See? You should have been given these tires yesterday, Mr. Stetson."

Derek inspected Carmen's tires which read Behemoth *Special Blend Race Slicks.*

"Race slicks? But we weren't on a clean paved track. Racing slicks would have torn themselves to shreds on a normal road." Derek questioned.

Mr. Sullivan shook his head, "Read the label, Mr. Stetson. It says 'Special Blend Race Slicks.' Behemoth has developed a tire with the same equivalent performance as a racing tire but the endurance of a road tire. You were using a regular semi-slick tire designed for a race half the size you competed in yesterday. I'm impressed you qualified at all."

Now Derek was just as furious as Mr. Sullivan, "So who gave me the wrong damn tires?"

Mr. Sullivan laughed almost maniacally under his breath while shaking his head, "I don't know Mr. Stetson, but I'll tell you what. This just jumped to the top of my to-do list, and I can assure you, someone is getting fired today."

Derek was taken aback, "Oh shit."

"Oh, about the racer in the Ford pickup. She was well within her rights to cut corners the way she did. There are no rules keeping someone from doing so. Now if she was cutting half of the track, then the Behemoth race board would confer and penalize accordingly. This isn't your standard race, Mr.

Stetson; almost anything goes here." Mr. Sullivan said reassuringly.

Conflicted, Derek agreed to the lack of rules.

"Who won yesterday anyway?" Derek asked Mr. Sullivan.

"Mr. Killian Briggs took the victory yesterday. Followed by Mr. Kareem Collins in his Mclaren Senna, and in third was Ms. Sandra Dorette in her Lamborghini Veneno. Would you like to see the entire leaderboard, sir?"

Derek agreed and took a form from Mr. Sullivan.

Driver Name – Driver Vehicle – Total Points

   1. K. Briggs – '18 Ferrari FXX-K Evo – 20 Points

   2. K. Collins – '18 McLaren Senna – 18 Points

   3. S. Dorette – '13 Lamborghini Veneno – 15 Points

   4. C. Winters – '94 Mazda Mx-5 Miata – 12 Points

   5. W. Stonewood – '16 Ford GT – 10 Points

   6. B. Rogers – '01 Nissan Skyline – 8 Points

   7. G. Fischer – '15 Koenigsegg One:1 – 5 Points

   8. S. Garcia – '23 Audi R8 – 4 Points

   9. L. Wilson – '17 Aston Martin DB9 – 3 Points

10. F. Price – '22 Mercedes AMG SL – 2 Points

11. C. Anderson – '11 Ford Raptor – 1 Point

12. D. Stetson – '69 Dodge Charger Daytona – No Points

Derek sighed, "Thank you, Mr. Sullivan, for all your help with the tires and the rule clarifications." I can breathe easier now."

Mr. Sullivan shared his gratitude for Derek's inquiries as he left to fire some Behemoth Technicians.

CHAPTER TWELVE

CHARLIE

SUNDAY, JULY 2, 2028

"Is you Mr. Derek Stetson?" someone said behind Derek.

Derek turned around, "Ya that's me. Can I help you?"

The man grinned, "Actually, I'm here to help you! My name is Charlie, and I'm a certified Behemoth Technician that's been assigned to help you with your mechanical needs. I've been certified in everything from high performance engine assembly to bodywork."

"Well, alrighty then, Charlie. Welcome aboard!" Derek said delightedly, "Why don't you help me with these tires then.

Even though Derek could do all the maintenance himself, he appreciated Charlie's help, especially with the heavy lifting. Plus, it gave him someone to talk to while they worked.

Charlie introduced himself more thoroughly as they worked on the Daytona's brake system. He was raised in

East Oklahoma on a small farm. He had to become a top-tier mechanic and body man because they couldn't afford to take their broken-down farm vehicles to a professional shop. He was a tall, lean man who was extremely strong even though he didn't look the part. In true farmer fashion, he always wore overalls and a straw hat.

"So what brings you out to Texas then Charlie?" Derek asked.

"Well, when I grew up, I went to one of those fancy trade schools out here in Texas and that's how I became a certified mechanic. Because I already knew just about ever'thing there was to know about cars, I passed with flying colors. That's when Behemoth picked me up and I've been a helper here ever since." Charlie replied.

"How many racers have you worked with?"

"Oh, about 10-20 different ones, I never really bothered keepin' count." Charlie chuckled, "Because of my lengthy time here, Behemoth even paid for some racing classes for me so I can be a crew chief too."

"So you're my crew chief too? Where were ya' at the first race? I could've used some help." Derek implored.

Charlie sighed, "Sorry sir, but because there was no pit stops in the first race, or the third race, I couldn't help you. The second race is the only one on a real track so I'm a part of your team." Charlie explained.

Charlie and Derek continued to inspect and repair anything they could find under the vehicle.

"You realize how bad your shocks are under here?" Charlie pointed out.

Derek headed towards the rear of the car where Charlie was standing. They both looked up at the rear shock absorbers; they were leaking.

"Well I'll be damned," Derek exclaimed as he rushed towards the front of the vehicle, "The fronts are just as bad!"

"That would explain the premature tire-wear in your last race," Charlie elaborated.

"Oh no, Mr. Sullivan explained that to me already," Derek interrupted, "They gave me the wrong tires."

"Wrong tires!? WRONG TIRES!?" Charlie burst into tears laughing, "Ooh, someone got fired today." Then, Charlie started coughing from laughing too hard, "Behemoth takes their tires *very* seriously."

After seeking out the free replacement shock absorbers from the Behemoth parts desk, Charlie and Derek started installing them. Then, they each took an end of the car and got to work.

"You given any thought about strategy for your next race?" Charlie pondered.

Derek set his ratchet down briefly and scratched his stubbled chin, "No, I haven't. Honestly, I don't know enough about the next course to strategize."

Charlie nodded in agreement, "Well, we're ahead of schedule anyway. After we tighten up these last bolts, let's take a look at that track."

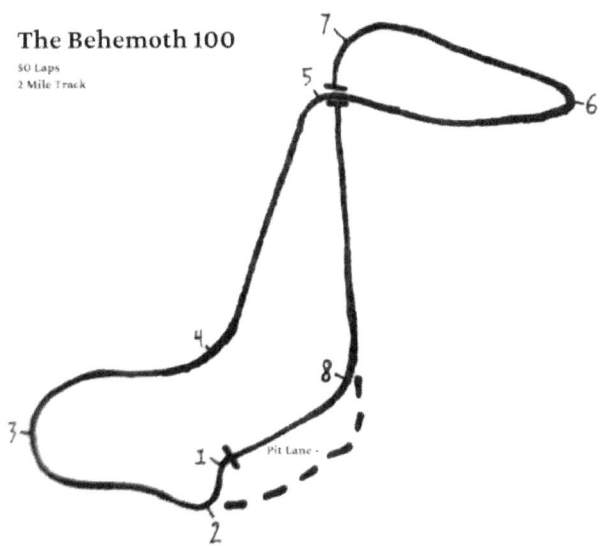

The Behemoth 100

50 Laps
2 Mile Track

Charlie and Derek hunched over the computer, staring at the next race track, taking in all the straights and curves. Strategizing this technical racetrack so Derek can redeem enough points for a comeback.

"Looks like you have 50 laps of this two mile circuit here," Charlie described.

Derek turned back towards the screen, "Shit, that's a long race."

"You're gonna have to keep a pace with this one," Charlie explained, "If you floor it in order to get laps ahead of everyone, you're gonna end up crashin' or breakin'. Most people wanna get in front, but there's always someone gonna sneak on ya from behind because they pitted earlier."

Derek shook his head in disbelief, "Damn, that makes sense. I wish you were my crew chief in the old days; I might have won something."

Charlie walked him through every inch of that track. Not telling him how to race it per se, but how people will respond to it.

"See here, these ain't your professional racecar drivers that you're used to; these be amateurs," Charlie pointed out, "Most of these fellers never seen the inside of a racing classroom. All they know is to go fast and as you discovered in the first race, most of them don't know where the brake pedal even is!"

Derek remembered the first sharp left corner on the last race; he had to practically pull over to let the amateurs run straight through the intersection and cause a massive pile-up.

"Man, this turn one and two is gonna have everyone all messed up," Charlie predicted, "You're comin' in hot from that last straightaway and final right turn to a damn-near dead stop to make that sharp left chicane!"

Derek noticed something else as well, "Not to mention turn six! I noticed everybody here struggles with the hairpins; I passed a few people there in the last race."

Charlie nodded, "Too true. Too true. Let's not forget turn eight. That fast corner is gonna throw some metal at the guard rails, I can guarantee that."

"So what's the strategy boss?" Derek asked Charlie.

"Well, fortunately for you, you're already in last place."

Derek was shocked, "Fortunately? How on God's green Earth is being in last a good thing?"

"Well Mr. High and Mighty," Charlie came back, "now you don't have to worry about anyone rear-ending ya in the corners! Believe you me, you have the best advantage of them all."

Derek raised an eyebrow, "Oh really."

Charlie's smile went from ear to ear, "Yes really, you get to learn off of every opponent in front of you! Some dumbass decides to brake too late, now you know. Someone takes a faster line, you steal it from him next lap. Being dead last is more of a blessing than a curse."

Derek thought about Charlie's words, and although it didn't make much sense, he accepted it. Take the good and the bad from everyone before him and use it all to his advantage. He'd also get more drafting opportunities in last place than if he were in front.

CHAPTER THIRTEEN

MISUNDERSTANDINGS

SUNDAY, JULY 2, 2028

Derek heard Carmen yell from across the bay, "Hey Cowboy! How's she holding up?"

"She's fine now that she got the right tires on her and the shocks have been replaced." Derek responded.

"So that's what was wrong? I was wondering why you were struggling yesterday. You passed everyone like it was nothing!"

"I wish that were true," Derek continued, "there were a couple of y'all that were a pain in the ass to pass."

Carmen's eyebrow rose, "Oh, really? Name one person who was a genuine challenge to pass for you; you have the best car here without question."

Derek chuckled at the compliment, "Thank you for thinking so, but I'm just a little bit more experienced than most of the people here is all. I'd be willing to bet that a lot of these supercars would beat my poor Daytona straight up in a heartbeat. As for your question, the lady in the Ford Raptor gave me a run for my money."

"Wait a minute, the huge pickup truck? That's who gave you trouble? REALLY!?" Carmen's pitch raised with every question.

"Yes, the pickup," Derek replied after rubbing his ears, "Even if we ignore the bullshit corner cutting, that truck took up the entire road when it started drifting. There wasn't a window to sneak through at all!"

"Sheesh, thank goodness I didn't have to deal with that, but then again, I had to deal with snobby Mc'Rich-face." Carmen angrily stated while crossing her arms.

"Oh yeah, Killian. What an asshole," Derek muttered, "What he did to Warren was despicable. I was lucky to make it through that!"

"Right!" Carmen yelled, "To make things worse, the tournament officials aren't doing a damn thing about it because Killian claimed it was an *accident*. What a..."

"I get it," Derek interrupted, "That's ridiculous. Anyway, how was the race for you?"

"Well, it went better than I expected. Learning the track was interesting; there were a lot of weird turns in there." Carmen explained.

Derek nodded, "I hear ya, like the corner leaving the suburbs; it looked like you could take it so much faster than you actually could."

"YES! I *hated* that one!" Carmen exclaimed. "I'm just happy that despite my transmission problems, I was able to stay competitive."

"You call that competitive!" came an annoyingly familiar voice.

Carmen and Derek collectively sighed and dropped their heads in disbelief.

"That's right, suckers! First place has arrived," Killian boasted.

They tried to ignore him unsuccessfully.

"I will admit though old man," Killian insultingly directed toward Derek, "your purple monster surprised me. The fact that this boat managed to stay planted in the corners with our fine-tuned supercars left me in awe."

Derek didn't know whether to be grateful for the compliment or insulted by everything else...

"You realize that this *boat* passed you with ease?" Derek returned.

"Oh please," Killian started laughing obnoxiously, "the only reason you passed me is because Warren's Ford got in the way!"

Carmen interjected, "You pit maneuvered him! You were entirely responsible for that crash!"

Derek shot up to intercept Carmen from decking Killian in the face.

"Easy there tiger, nobody is at fault here okay," Killian unsuccessfully reassured, "Contact happens in racing babe, sheesh."

With Derek still holding Carmen back, Killian nonchalantly walked back to his stall.

Derek had to ensure she was calm before letting her go, "You good? Can I let you go?"

Carmen eased up and stopped struggling, "Yeah, Cowboy, you can let go now. I'm cool."

Before Derek could blink, Carmen broke loose of his arms and ran towards Killian's stall.

Derek sighed, "Damn it," and ran after her.

Killian never knew what hit him.

"Hey, pea-brain!" Carmen shouted.

As soon as Killian turned around, Carmen's fist landed square on his cheekbone, causing him to fall. At this point, Derek caught up to Carmen and stood between the two of them once more.

"Are you out of your mind Carmen!" Derek reasoned, "Do you realize that there are cameras everywhere and you'll be lucky if you aren't disqualified now!?"

Carmen took a step back, "Shit."

"Yeah, SHIT!" Derek yelled, "Now apologize to him right now before you cause any more damage."

Carmen helped Killian off the floor, "I'm sorry for socking you in the face," she said begrudgingly.

Killian responded, "It's alright, sweetheart, I'm just sorry...."

"Oh no you don't!" Derek interrupted, "you need to sincerely apologize to her and me as well! You directly insulted both of us and nobody appreciates a sore winner. Do you understand!?"

Killian realized he was out of his element and had no real influence over Derek.

"I apologize to both of you. I should not have insulted either of you or your cars. I will work on being more humble from here on out."

Derek put his arms down, "What's your deal man?"

Killian sat down on a shop stool and looked towards his Ferrari.

Carmen and Derek looked confused; he just pulled a complete one-eighty on them. He went from the overly confident, tall, handsome billionaire to a slouched, hopeless, and broken man in the corner.

Carmen leaned towards Derek and whispered, "What the hell just happened?"

Derek was equally stunned. He whispered, "I have no clue, but I'm going to find out."

Derek cautiously stepped towards Killian, who was now crying into his palms.

"Killian?" Derek opened, "It's Derek. Can you tell me what's going on?"

Killian didn't move as his breathing sped up.

"Oh shit," Derek muttered to himself.

Carmen forgot about the petty feud and became very concerned, "What?"

Derek turned towards Carmen, "He's starting to have a panic attack."

"What do we do?!" Carmen asked anxiously.

Derek immediately answered, "First of all, you need to stay calm too. We don't need two meltdowns at a time now do we?"

Carmen immediately calmed down, sat beside Killian on the next stool, and placed her hand on his back. Now that Carmen was cared for, Derek could focus on Killian.

"Killian?" Derek asked, "Can you talk to me buddy?"

Killian shook his head no.

"Okay, you're having a panic attack man," he explained, "have you had these before?"

Killian nodded.

"Do you take medicine for it?

No.

"Okay, we need you to calm down. Can you slow down your breathing for me" Derek asked.

Killian nodded, and Derek walked him through deep breathing techniques, eventually calming him down.

"Thank you," Killian said, exhausted.

Carmen and Derek stood up.

"You need rest. I'll check in on you tomorrow," Derek reassured.

CHAPTER FOURTEEN

CROSS-THREADED

MONDAY, JULY 3, 2028

Derek knocked on the hotel room door. A very disheveled Killian Briggs answered.

"Good God, man!" Derek exclaimed, "It looks like you fell in the trenches in WWI."

Killian scoffed, "Nice to see you too, sheriff."

"So, you wanna fill me in on what happened yesterday?"

Killian proceeded to tell Derek about his anxiety career. Coming from a wealthy family, he never had a want for anything as a child. However, his parents were brutal. His mother was a lawyer, and his father was a surgeon. Even though they divorced when he was in fifth grade, Killian's parents seemed perfect. Nothing Killian did was good enough for them, especially since Killian decided to pursue a career in motorsports. Finally, after many years of trying to convince him to change his career, his parents gave up on him and gave him a hefty allowance to get Killian to leave them alone.

"Sheesh man, that's awful!" Derek said, flabbergasted.

Killian responded, "Tell me about it."

He continued to explain to Derek that because of his parents' ignorance, Killian's mental stability spiraled out of control. He had to chase perfection to gain their affection that never came. He used his vast wealth to '*partner*' with Ferrari and pursue perfection. His relationship with Ferrari caused Behemoth to invite Killian to the tournament. Provided Killian kept financially supporting Ferrari, they'd provide Killian with a car of his choice for the tournament, as long as it was a Ferrari.

Derek shook his head, "So all these years, you've been chasing perfection. You realize that's an impossible goal right?"

Killian rejected Derek's wisdom, "I refuse to believe that. I can prove to my asshole parents that I can achieve perfection, just like them. No, better than them!"

"No wonder your head is screwed on wrong," Derek sighed. "Look kid, your parents ain't perfect I can guarantee you that. Wait, they are human right?"

Killian glared at Derek, "Yes, they're human smartass."

"Hey, just checking," Derek laughed with his hands up, "to be honest, everyone around here in this tournament looks at you with resentment because they all believe you have a perfect life."

Killian looked up, confused, "How is my life possibly perfect?"

"Oh come on! Parent drama aside, you have it made! You have more money than you know what to do with. You drive a kickass Ferrari, and you are constantly acting as if you're the king of the world!"

Killian shook his head in disbelief, "No, I have to act that way because perfection requires confidence."

"How much do you want to bet your parents are thinking the same thing?" Derek questioned.

In tears, Killian asked, "Why are you being so nice to me? Why are you trying to help?"

After taking a second to formulate a response, Derek replied, "Because I try to be a decent human being, not a perfect one, a good one. Plus, if anyone can help you, it's me. Because of my big crash back in the day, the doctors say I suffer from PTSD, and I go through very similar attacks to yours."

Killian was set back, "You do?"

"Yeah, I hit a wall over a hundred miles per hour while rolling. Look, I don't really dream much, but when I do, it's always of the crash."

Killian became concerned, "May I ask what happened?"

"Sure kid."

Derek proceeded to explain to Killian that it was the championship race, and Derek needed the win to claim his first-ever title. He was pushing his Corvette past its limits trying to catch up to the leader. Finally, victory was within his grasp. With five laps to go, his crew chief said that he was long overdue at the pits, but Derek knew if he pitted then, he would lose a lap on his opponents, and it would be game over, so Derek pushed through. On the last lap, Derek was bumper-to-bumper with Porsche in first place.

Using his slipstream, he rushed past him on the outside with a slingshot maneuver. Unfortunately, Derek miscalculated, and even though he comfortably passed the Porsche, he ran wide in the next corner and ran right into the marbles. When Derek realized his error, his tire had blown to shreds. The car jerked into the infield and caught air.

Derek had to stop his story, "I'm sorry kid, I can't go on."

Killian looked mortified, "So you've never won?"

On the verge of tears, Derek shook his head no.

"I guess we are more alike than I thought," Killian realized, "We both want to win and redeem our past."

"That's true kid, but do you want to know the difference between us?" Derek asked.

"You have a heck of a lot more experience than I do?"

Derek chuckled, "Besides that! I know what I'm racing for. Yes, redemption for my failed career would be amazing. But I'm doing this for my family first and foremost. We need the money so we can pay our bills, and give our daughter the life she deserves. What are you racing for Killian?"

Killian didn't know the answer, "Uhm, I guess you'd be pretty mad at me if I said perfection wouldn't you?"

Derek gave Killian a stern look.

"Okay okay! I'll think about it." Killian admitted.

Derek laughed, "Well, you better figure it out soon kid because racing without a motive is like shooting with a blank bullet. It sounds loud and impressive, but at the end of the day, you aren't shooting anything."

CHAPTER FIFTEEN

FEELING THE PRESSURE

SATURDAY, JULY 8, 2028

"Mic. check, one, one, two, two, anybody listenin' over?" Yelled Charlie.

"Jeez Charlie," Derek exclaimed, "I'm here and I can hear you LOUD and clear!"

"Sorry 'bout that boss, just checkin' the systems."

Derek was in the Daytona doing his checks as well.

"I got the right tires this time right Charlie?" Derek asked to ensure he had a fair playing field this time around.

Charlie laughed hysterically, "YESSIR! You got them fancy Behemoth slicks this time. This beaut' is all good, inside and out!"

Derek sighed in relief.

"Real question is how are you holding up?" Charlie asked.

Derek was confused, "Uh, fine I guess. Why do you ask?"

"I did some more research and I come across your accident," Charlie explained, "Then it all made sense to me; why you froze last race. So I'm gonna ask again, you okay?"

Derek paused, "I'm nervous, but I'm okay."

"Good, I don't wanna freak you out or nothin' but I need to remind you that you gotta get at least fifth to qualify for the next round," Charlie informed Derek, "And if you end up getting fifth, you won't be doing yourself any favors points-wise."

Derek understood and was about to respond when he heard a voice over the loudspeaker... "DRIVERS! START. YOUR. ENGINES!"

The crowd's roar was quickly drowned out by the earth-shattering sounds of engines firing up. Derek looked to his left to see the windows on the neighboring building dancing to the racers' song. With his adrenaline pumping, Derek revved his engine in anticipation.

The racers followed the pace car to the track. This was a crucial time for Derek because he needed to learn the way. Leaving pit row and entering the straightaway after turn two, Derek saw all the cars in front of him, "Alright, Derek, patience. Charlie's right. Wait for them to make their mistakes and utilize them."

"Aw, shucks!" Charlie wept, "That was the most beautiful sentiment I ever heard."

"Oh, son of a...." Derek swore, "My mic was on, wasn't it?"

"HA-HA! Yessir! And it was recorded too. You already know that's gonna be my new ringtone, "Charlie's Right,"" Charlie laughed hysterically.

Cruising around turn three, Derek noticed that the Ford Raptor in front of him was already sliding into this relatively fast corner.

"You seeing this Charlie? This truck is all over the place!" Derek commented.

"Easy now Mr. Stetson," Charlie reassured, "I have a feeling that once you pass 'er, you won't have to worry about 'er passing you in this race; there's no room to corner cut in this track."

Derek shrugged, "Touche."

Ahead was turn six, the hairpin that Charlie warned Derek about.

"Damn son!" Charlie exclaimed, "We ain't even racing yet and you got a bunch of rookies running wide in the hairpin. You'll get a lot of positions there, I tell you what!"

After completing the hairpin, they took a sharp left ninety under the bridge and entered the biggest straightaway.

"This here's the most dangerous straight son. People are gonna try and take turn eight flat out, which is entirely doable, but then they'll be goin' too fast for turn one!" Charlie reminded.

Instead of taking turn eight with the rest of the racers, the pace car went straight into the pit lane, marking the start of the race.

Rounding the final corner, Derek spotted the green flag waving and everyone else flooring it.

"Remember what we done talked about Derek, hold back." Charlie shouted over the comms.

Derek did as he was told and saw everything before his eyes. The Mercedes AMG, in sixth place, hit the first apex beautifully, then as he went straight toward the second corner, his right-front bumper clipped the wall and caused him to spin out in the tight corner. The Koenigsegg 1:1 in seventh barely escaped with only cosmetic paint damage, but being unable to stop in time, the Audi R8 T-boned the Mercedes going equally fast through the corner. Then, unfortunately, the Aston Martin DB9 joined the carnage by rear-ending the Audi. The yellow flag immediately flew, and the R34 Skyline, Ford Raptor, and Derek's Dodge Daytona completely stopped.

"OH SHIT!" Charlie swore, "I knew it was gon' be a bad one but HOT DAMN. On lap one of all things. Well, good news Derek! You don't have to worry about passing those folks. They're toast, even the Aston!"

Derek's eyes were wide, "I'm glad I didn't book it ahead like the rest of them."

Charlie laughed, "See, I ain't as crazy as you think!"

"I wouldn't go that far old man," Derek countered, "You're just the right kind of crazy."

"Whelp," Charlie sighed, "maybe we can actually start racing in a little bit once they clean this mess up."

It didn't take long for the clean-up crew to do their jobs, and the race was back on. The race officials claimed the accident was a *false start*, so everyone was still on lap one. Immediately, Derek saw a difference in strategy from the drivers entering turn one. They nearly stopped completely entering the corner as they weaved through the technical chicane.

Heading onto the first straightaway, Derek asked Charlie, "Am I still pacing?"

"Boy, you better be pacing for the next 20 laps at least!" Charlie shouted, "The only people I want you passing is the Ford Raptor n'front of you and the Nissan n'front of her! Preferably this lap too! Keep pace with the back of the leading pack; you don't want to get lapped!"

"Yes sir!" Derek replied.

By the time Charlie had given his speech, Derek and the Raptor were at the hairpin. Looking like he was about to roll over, the Ford lifted his driver's side front tire as he power-slid the corner wide. Derek didn't hesitate. Keeping all four tires firmly planted on the tarmac, he hit the apex hard and passed the truck on the inside. After passing the Ford, Derek caught up to the Skyline in turn seven but couldn't pass him there. But ahead was the big straightaway, and Derek knew he had more horsepower than his opponent. He could hear the Skyline's throttle open wide, so Derek returned the favor. Shifting down, the Daytona launched forward and forced Derek into his seat. As much as the poor Nissan tried, it simply couldn't keep up with the HEMI in the Daytona. Rounding the final corner, Derek slowed down to safely maneuver the tight chicane ahead.

"Congratulations!" Charlie announced, "You did what you were told. Now you just gotta survive fourty-nine more laps of that against cars that are actually competitive."

CHAPTER SIXTEEN

ENDURANCE

SATURDAY, JULY 8, 2028

"Alright Derek," Charlie started, "here's where strategy is gonna get you farther than speed. I want you to shift a grand before redline to conserve fuel!"

Derek was shocked, "Wait what? Even the pickup will catch up to me at that pace!"

"No he ain't! Trust your car kid, because nobody else here does!" Charlie shouted.

Since Charlie was so adamant about this strategy, Derek begrudgingly obliged. He kept shifting early and saving fuel while barely seeing his opponents ahead of him. Even at slightly slower speeds, Derek was making good time. The Skyline and the Raptor were nowhere to be seen, which was a good sign, but Derek needed to catch up on the opponents ahead of him.

"Charlie?" Derek asked, "You realize that everyone ahead of me is in multimillion dollar supercars and pushing them to their absolute limit?"

As usual, Charlie laughed hysterically at the ridiculous question, "Oh my boy! Of course, I know that! Why else would I tell you to slow down?!"

"What the hell does that supposed to mean?!" Derek shouted back in frustration.

"Son, none of them fellers know the limits of the cars they're driving! You really think they're gonna survive another forty-five laps out there kid?!"

Derek shut up for a minute and realized the truth behind Charlie's words. Derek knew that he wasn't pushing his car near as hard as it could handle, and judging by the lack of competition surrounding him, everyone else was.

Derek spent the next five laps completely alone. According to Charlie, the Skyline and the Raptor were too busy battling for eighth place to focus on catching up with the rest of the pack, and the same was true for the group out front; they were so focused on battling for positions that they all were sabotaging each others' lap times. On the other hand, Derek practiced his racing lines every second of every lap. Even though he was still following Charlie's orders and keeping it slow, Derek was the only one on the field improving his lap times. To Derek's astonishment, he started approaching the Koenigsegg 1:1!

"Charlie!" Derek shouted, "Are you seeing what I'm seeing?"

"Yessir, I do!" Charlie laughed, "While you were driving clean and paced, Mr. One to One kept his pedal on the floor and neglected his brakes! I bet you can guess what kind of problems he's having right now."

Derek looked at his dashboard, "I'd be willing to bet the same problems I'm having because I'm on a quarter tank, Charlie!"

"Oh relax! You ain't the only one. In fact, Ms. Miata just pit and is filling up her tank as well!"

"Okay Charlie, what's the plan then?"

"Here's whatcha gonna do, these supercars are not gonna pit on the tenth lap like the Miata did. I don't want you to pit until after that Koenigsegg does in front of you."

Derek was flabbergasted, "I'm sorry, what? Who even knows how much gas that guy even has?"

"Well, I do, ya worry wart! Team one-to-one is losing their shit in the stall next to us. You have a quarter tank; it sounds to me that he has a gas light on."

Sure enough, Derek quickly caught up to the Koenigsegg due to his opponent's fuel shortage. Approaching the final corner, Derek's opponent went into the pits.

"Mister Stetson!" Charlie shouted, "How's your tires?!"

"I haven't noticed any loss of grip, why?" Derek responded.

Charlie chuckled, "I'm looking at the tires that the Koenigsegg just took off and replaced and they look brand spanking new! These tires are legit!"

"Okay? So what's your point?" Derek asked.

"Son, you keep going until your needle hits zero, and when you come in for fuel, that's all you're getting!"

"That's asking for disaster! What are you thinking?!"

"Were you not listening knucklehead?! The Koenigsegg's tires aren't worn in the slightest after ten laps! What makes you think yours are?"

Derek paused and realized what Charlie was saying, so he kept pressing on. He was about halfway through lap eleven when Charlie notified him that the Koenigsegg was back out and looking for him.

"Alright Derek, I know it might seem scary, but you need to keep your current pace."

Derek swore, "Damn it Charlie, he's going to catch up!"

"Son, you caught up to him in eleven laps and you still have thirty-nine to go. Does it sound like I'm worried if he's gonna catch back up to you? Just do it again!"

There was a pause.

"Derek, we have a game changer."

"Okay? Care to tell me what it is?" Derek responded in an irritated tone.

"Four of the five cars in front of you are pitting!" Charlie elaborated.

"Who's the fifth" Derek asked.

"The Mazda," Charlie answered, "because she already pit before."

Derek slammed on the gas, "I'm two corners away, I'll see you in a second."

"You better get here sooner than that boy! They're all taking their tires off right now!" Charlie screamed.

Derek arrived at the pits as quickly as he was allowed. One of Charlie's pit crew members checked the tires and reassured Derek that they were still flawless, and it took no time to fill up the Daytona with fuel. By the time Derek was ready to go, so were the supercars in front of him.

"Alrighty then." Charlie exclaimed, "That was a good stop. You ready for some news that you've been waiting to hear?"

Derek's interest peaked, "Go on."

"It's time to slightly change our strategy. The new plan is to keep pace with these four doofuses here."

"Hey genius!" Derek shouted, "I can't keep up with these guys if I'm still keeping my revs low!"

Charlie laughed at Derek's confusion, "Son, I don't give a rat's ass about your rpms now. Just keep pace with these four, and do NOT pass them all. The new strategy is for them to pay for your gas!"

Derek chuckled at the remark. The new plan was to stay in the supercars' slipstreams, which would improve speed and fuel economy with a fraction of the work.

With the new plan set, Derek shifted down a gear and floored it.

CHAPTER SEVENTEEN

TENSION

SATURDAY, JULY 8, 2028

L ap fifteen: Everyone was feeling the pressure. The race was still young, and anyone could take the lead. Carmen had a commanding lead, nearly a lap ahead of everyone. Derek was still in sixth place while keeping pace with the McLaren, Ferrari, Lamborghini, and Ford.

Charlie said, "Hey Derek, I got a bad feeling in my gut here bud."

"What does that supposed to mean Charlie?"

"I don't know!" he shouted, "Get out of sixth and get to a qualifying position."

Derek was confused, "So you want me to pass now?"

"Not all the way. Keep yourself in at least fifth, but continue our slipstream plan."

Finally understanding what he was trying to tell him, Derek, passed the Ford GT and got behind the Lamborghini Veneno. Looking in his rearview, he noticed that the

Ford wasn't the only opponent behind him anymore; the Koenigsegg 1:1 had finally caught back up. The Koenigsegg's driver did not look pleased either. In an attempt to pass, he used the GT's slipstream to slingshot his way past Derek.

"Oh shit," Derek swore.

Charlie was also shocked, "Hot damn kid, that guy really doesn't like you, does he?"

"Well I did pass him with a muscle car that's just under half a century older than his car."

"HA!! You tell 'em!" Charlie yelled in enjoyment, "Alright, he just stole fifth from ya so let's piss him off some more shall we?"

Derek chuckled, "Yes sir!"

Approaching the big straight before the last turn, Derek started teasing the Koenigsegg. By keeping pace with him, Derek placed the Daytona's nose a paper's width away from the Koenigsegg's rear bumper. He tried to pull away, but Derek kept up with a fraction of the work; he was engulfed in his opponent's slipstream. They were right on top of the last corner, and Derek eased off the gas to allow them both to safely make it. Just as they left turn eight, Derek launched past the Koenigsegg on the outside. This angered his opponent something fierce. When Derek hit the brakes for the first chicane, the Koenigsegg cut him off, leading him wide into the second corner. Predicting this would happen, Derek slowed down to allow the mistake, just to hit the gas just as quickly so he could pass him on the inside and leave the Koenigsegg in the dust.

Derek could hear Charlie whooping through his headset, "That's right my boy! Now that's racing right there!"

Derek laughed at Charlie's remark.

"Alright son, you need to pass that Lambo in front of ya because that one to one driver probably has smoke comin' out his ears."

"Where should I be Charlie?" Derek asked.

"Try for third place at least, and don't get behind fifth. If we stay in that margin, we might have a chance at pulling this off."

Nodding his head to himself, Derek pushed on. After two laps, Derek finally passed the Veneno. Fortunately, after that, the Koenigsegg lost sixth place to the Ford. This left Derek with the daunting task of passing Killian's Ferrari to gain third place.

Five more laps passed, and all six drivers swapped places with each other numerous times. Now, Derek found his way into third place behind the Mclaren Senna, followed by the Ford, Lamborghini, Killian's Ferrari, and the Koenigsegg, and they were all low on fuel.

"I'm under a quarter tank Charlie!" Derek shouted at his crew chief.

"Hold your position, Stetson!" Charlie returned, "We gotta wait these super-babies out a little longer!"

Unfortunately for Derek, he was in a giant game of fuel chicken; who would pit first? Coming out of the chicane on lap twenty-four, everyone was bunched up together. They battled for positions through each corner and each straight. Nobody held a place for longer than ten seconds. Then, around turn seven, Derek noticed his rear tires started sliding.

"Sorry Charlie, I gotta pit. I can feel my tires giving!"

Charlie sighed, "It's okay, kid; we'll catch back up in the second half.

Derek was bumper to bumper with the McLaren when his opponent's engine suddenly exploded next to the Daytona! The Senna swerved and bumped Derek's quarter panel, causing him to spin out of control. All the drivers slammed on their brakes as hard as they could and skidded out of the way of the spinning McLaren. After saving his car from rotating a complete three-sixty, Derek regained control and immediately entered the pit lane. To Derek's surprise, so did everyone else.

Derek pulled into his stall while the crew began fuelling his car and replacing his tires.

"Damn, Charlie! Is she okay?!"

Charlie looked concerned, "Don't know yet, buddy. Looked like a head gasket. That was a scary one."

Charlie directed his stare toward the track.

"What's that look for? He'll be okay."

"I'm sure Mr. Collins is okay. That's not my concern." Charlie said as he pointed towards the track.

Derek saw her too. Carmen wasn't pitting again, placing her a full lap ahead of everyone.

"No shame in second there Derek" Charlie reassured.

With the tires back on, the pit crew hastily removed the fuel pump, spilling some on the floor. The heat from the brakes caused the fuel to ignite.

Charlie screamed, "Derek! Get the hell out of there!"

Seeing the flames in his rearview mirror, Derek quickly undid his safety harness and jolted out of the vehicle. When he exited the car, Derek was mortified by what he saw. His teammate, Michael, fueling the vehicle, had spilled it onto his pant leg and was on fire. Because it was racing fuel, it took no time for the fire to climb up to his torso. The entire team rushed to his aid, throwing fire blankets over him and having him roll on the ground. In excruciating pain, the man screamed for his life.

CHAPTER EIGHTEEN

FROM THE FLAMES

SATURDAY, JULY 8, 2028

E veryone was panicking.

"Goddamn it, somebody call the medics!" Charlie shouted.

Derek rushed to a neighboring stall and pointed at the crew chief, "You! Call the medics!" Then he ran back to his tortured teammate and overheard Charlie.

"Derek, the Car!"

Looking over, he realized that the Daytona's quarter panel was still on fire. Derek grabbed the nearest fire extinguisher and attacked the fire. It was no use. The fire wasn't dissipating.

"Shit, GET CLEAR!" Derek screamed while running away.

The team started to clear the area when the gas tank blew, sending everyone flying through the air. Since Derek was the closest to the car, he felt the explosion the worst. Fortunately for Derek, he was still wearing his flame-proof racing suit, so extinguishing the fire on himself was easy.

"Derek!" Charlie screamed, "Derek!" He raced towards him, "Derek! You all right?"

Derek was dazed, and his ears were ringing. He groaned in pain.

"Derek, how many fingers am I holding up?" Charlie asked while holding up four fingers.

Derek raised his hands with four fingers extended.

The on-site paramedics finally arrived, and the fire department put out the fire. They took Michael to the on-site hospital since he was in critical condition. The rest of the first responders were tasked with the rest of the team, starting with Derek. The medic assigned to Derek concluded that the primary blast caused moderate damage to his eardrums and a minor concussion and that it would have been a lot worse if he hadn't started running away. Fortunately, he didn't receive any secondary blast injuries, such as shrapnel and debris, but Derek did get a lot of bruises due to being thrown from the explosion. Provided he took the time to rest and heal, Derek would be fine within a few days.

The race officials waved the red flag and stopped the race because of the explosion and the injuries. Even though Derek and the rest of his team would make it, they had yet to hear about Micheal's condition. Derek was sitting on the K-rails on pit lane, completely zoned out, when Carmen approached him and patted him on the shoulder gently.

"Hey, you okay?"

Derek had to refocus before he could answer, "Hm? Oh, hey Carmen. Ya, I'm fine. Just a little banged up is all, and my ears hurt like hell."

"Jeez, I can imagine."

"I'll tell you one thing. I did *not* feel like a superhero walking away from an exploding car."

Trying to hold back laughter, Carmen replied, "Oh brother. You sound like my husband."

"Oh ya? How's he doing?"

Carmen's expression fell, "Oh. He died a couple years back."

"I'm sorry. I didn't know."

"It's okay. There's no way you could have known. He died in a training exercise in his F-35."

"Air-Force?" Derek asked.

"25 years. He was amazing."

"Sounds like it." Derek tried to change the subject, "How'd the race go for you? I don't even remember seeing you."

"Man, it was fantastic. Nobody could touch my acceleration. I felt alive."

"I hear ya. I always feel most alive when I'm behind the wheel."

"You know, before it blew up trying to kill you," Carmen laughed.

"Alright smart-alec," Derek chuckled as he lightly shoved her shoulder.

Just as the mood started recovering, Killian sat down next to them.

"You good?" Killian asked.

"Ya man. I'm fine."

"You hear about the quitters?"

Carmen interjected, "Quitters?"

"Ya. The Skyline and the Raptor are out. They were saying that the race was *unbalanced* and *unfair*. Whatever."

Derek thought about it briefly before responding, "It makes sense why they would forfeit. I was told there were no class divisions and there would be a bunch of diversity, but all I see are supercars, Carmen's Miata, and myself."

Killian gave an aggressive "HA! It's because they're too slow. They all got disqualified in the first round."

Then suddenly, the three heard a voice behind them, "That's rich. It used to be the other way around!"

All three turned around simultaneously to see Warren approaching them, "It wasn't that long ago that the supercars were the ones falling behind. How's your team, Stetson?"

"They're okay, just worried for Micheal."

"That sucks man. I can't even imagine what that's like," Warren said, shaking his head.

They were interrupted by Mr. Sullivan calling everyone to the center of the road so he could give an announcement.

"Alright ladies and gents, I have all the answers you're looking for. First and foremost, the young lad, Michael, who was fueling up Mr. Stetson's car is alive and stable, however the doctors say that he will be crippled for the rest of his life due to the severity of the burns."

The crowd was silent, for everyone was holding back tears.

"Secondly, I have the results from this race in my hand right here," he said, waving a piece of paper.

Killian was visibly angry, "What do you mean results?! We didn't even finish the race!"

"Mr. Briggs, settle down please so I can ex...."

"I will not settle down, this is unfair!"

"MR. BRIGGS! Did you not see the red flag?" Mr. Sullivan yelled, "Due to the circumstances of this race, it is entirely fair to cut it short. May I continue your royal heinie?!"

He took a sarcastic bow toward Killian without breaking eye contact, causing Killian to shut up. "Thank you. Now, the race committee has agreed that the finish line starting lap twenty-five marks the end of the race. So Mrs. Winters, congratulations; you took first place!"

The crowd politely clapped.

Then Killian interrupted again, "Lap twenty-five? The rest of us didn't even cross the line yet!"

"Do you ever shut up Killian?" Roared Mr. Sullivan, "I was just about to explain that to you... Since, like our registered nincompoop so delicately brought up, the rest of you technically didn't cross the finish line for lap twenty-four, your positions will be determined by who entered the pits first. So, Mr. Stetson, congratulations, you took second place! Followed by Mr. Stonewood in Third. Ms. Dorette placed fourth and Mr. Briggs placed fifth. Everyone else, I apologize to inform you that you did not qualify, but you can watch the rest of the competition free of charge. The tournament standings will be posted at the garage. Thank you all, and try to get some rest tonight."

CHAPTER NINETEEN

PERSPECTIVE

SATURDAY, JULY 8, 2028

"Hello?"

"Derek Stetson! You are in a heap of trouble!"

"Woah woah woah honey," Derek reassured, "everyone is okay!"

Shannon yelled into her phone, "Damn it Stetson, you traumatized our poor Daughter!" Derek could hear her change from angrily shouting to sobbing, "We thought you died."

"Oh, honey."

"They cut the broadcast when the man caught fire. Then, when they thought everything was okay and resumed the broadcast...." Shannon paused, holding back tears; she said, "we saw the Daytona blow!" Shannon started wailing.

"Honey, I'm okay. I promise on my life that I'm okay. Just a mild concussion and a couple of bruises."

"You can't scare us like that honey."

Derek couldn't get over hearing his wife crying over the phone, "Trust me, I didn't want to honey. I'm just as scared as you!"

Shannon sniffed and wiped away her tears, "I know honey. Are you going to be okay?"

"I think so."

Shannon sighed, "How's your teammate?"

"Michael? He's breathing, but the doctor said that the burns are going to leave him crippled for the rest of his life."

"That's awful! Just remember, it is not your fault."

Derek was now fighting back his own tears, "I can't help but feel responsible."

"Hey, cut that out right now! You are not responsible for this. It was a freak accident and nobody is at fault!"

Derek and Shannon were interrupted by a little voice in the background, "Momma, is that daddy?"

"Little miss, you are supposed to be in bed young lady."

Choking up tears, Derek asked, "Can I talk to her, please?"

Shannon handed her the phone.

"Hello?"

"Hi my little Autumn leaf. How's my baby doing?"

"I'm scared daddy."

"Oh, I know honey. I was scared too."

"Did you die?!" Autumn wailed.

"No honey," Derek chuckled through tears, "I didn't die. Just got a couple boo-boos."

"I wish I could kiss them all better," Autumn sniffed.

"I wish that too, honey."

"How's your friend, daddy?"

Holding back tears, Derek calmly responded, "He's okay honey. He's really hurt badly, but he's okay."

Sniffing, Autumn shook her head in acknowledgment.

"Hey, honey? Can I talk to mommy again, please?"

"Sure, Daddy. Momma! Daddy wants to talk to you again." Autumn shouted.

"I love you, my Autumn Leaf," Derek said while fighting back tears.

"I love you too, Daddy."

"Give momma a hug for me, okay?"

Autumn gave her momma a hug and handed her the phone.

"Hi, honey."

Derek couldn't hold back anymore; he started crying violently. "I don't know if I can keep going."

"Hey, don't talk like that honey. Breathe." Shannon reassured, "I know you're scared, but you are okay. You are safe! Say it."

"I am safe," Derek muttered as he kept crying.

"No sir. Say it like you mean it!"

"I am safe!" Derek shouted. "I miss you so much, my love."

"I miss you too honey. Do you want to walk me through the last race?"

Derek described the last race in perfect detail to his wife. How the car gave him the greatest adrenaline high of his life, how Charlie's strategy worked, and his fantastic pit crew.

"What the hell am I supposed to do without a car? The Daytona is pretty much totaled!"

"Don't worry about that now. You need sleep. You can figure out the details tomorrow. Deal?"

Derek sighed... Deal."

CHAPTER TWENTY

FROM THE ASHES

SUNDAY, JULY 9, 2028

D erek was in his stall staring at his destroyed Daytona. It looked like it lost a battle with a tank. The frame was bent like a bowl, hardly any sheet metal behind the A-pillar survived, the interior was burnt to nothing, and all the glass was shattered. It was beyond repair. No matter how many free parts Behemoth could offer.

From his stool, Derek heard Charlie's footsteps approach.

With a sullen expression, Charlie sat beside Derek, "How're you holdin' up, Stetson?"

Derek had no words, just a blank expression as he stared at his destroyed pride and joy.

Charlie took a deep breath, "I figured I should be the one to tell you that Michael passed away last night in his sleep."

Derek's head dropped between his hands and knees in despair.

"I'm sorry to be the bearer of bad news son, I really am," Charlie sighed.

Derek sat up and rubbed his eyes dry, "I think I need to quit Charlie."

"Quit? Why?"

"I completely traumatized my family last night! I can't put them through that again!"

"Son, you put in so much work. You can't stop now!"

Charlie reached into his pocket to show Derek the tournament standings.

Name – Vehicle – Total Points

1. Carmen Winters – '94 Mazda Mx-5 Miata – 32 Points

2. Killian Briggs – '18 Ferrari FXX-K Evo – 30 Points

3. Sandra Dorette – '13 Lamborghini Veneno – 27 Points

4. Warren Stonewood – '16 Ford GT – 25 Points

5. Derek Stetson – '69 Dodge Charger Daytona – 18 Points

"Right now, you may be in last, but you ain't out yet, damn it!" Charlie yelled.

"Charlie, that would take a miracle!"

"I've seen people come from worse. They gave the last race hell like I know you will."

"Hey buddy. I hate to break it to you, but do you see a functioning car here?! I can't win without a damn car!"

"Gee, I was hoping you'd bring that up," Charlie chuckled as he pulled out a pamphlet from his other pocket.

Derek took the pamphlet from him. It read in big, bold letters, "Loaner Cars."

"Hold on a second. You mean to tell me that Behemoth just has a bunch of cars lying around here that they're willing to throw away?"

"I'd hardly call it throwin' it away if they giving it to you; a top five finalist." Charlie explained.

Derek flipped through the options that were presented to him. It was filled with the latest European supercars and even a few electric ones.

"Nevermind, I don't stand a chance in any of these," Derek complained to Charlie, "I don't know anything about them!"

Charlie nodded, "Oh I think there's one car in particular that you'd appreciate. I even took the liberty of circlin' it for ya."

Derek continued to flip through the pages when suddenly, he saw the big, obnoxious, red circle that Charlie had drawn.

"Oh, that doesn't suck," Derek said in shock.

Charlie slapped his knee while laughing, "I told you so!"

"Alright, Charlie, I'll race. I can do some damage with this."

"Damn straight you can!"

"I'm going to win this race!" Derek declared, "For my family! And for Michael!"

The following Wednesday, Derek met Mrs. Barnes at an abandoned airport where Behemoth Parts had used an old aircraft hangar for storage.

"How are you holding up Mr. Stetson?"

"I'm hanging in there. Is this Santa's workshop?"

"More like Santa's showroom," Nora chuckled as she opened the door.

Derek's eyes lit up like a Christmas tree. The entire hangar could fit a C-17 cargo plane, filled to the brim with high-performance supercars.

"Oh wow!" Derek exclaimed, "This is heaven."

"I know right? Well, Charlie says you have already got one of these beauties in mind?"

"Oh Mrs. Barnes, you have no idea."

As Nora directed Derek towards the car located across the hangar.

"She was buried deep in the maze of cars when we got the news so we spent all of yesterday playing reverse Tetris to get her out and to the front of the hangar for you."

Derek saw what he was after.

It was a metallic, gunmetal grey 2016 Dodge Viper ACR with blacked-out trim.

Derek had to keep himself from drooling. "She's beautiful!"

"You think she's beautiful now? Pop the hood."

Derek followed her instructions and revealed an 8.5 Liter V10 that had clearly had work done because it was painted to match the vehicle's exterior paint and had two giant turbos connected to it.

Derek's jaw dropped to the floor, "It's so clean! How many horses does this thing produce?"

"The dyno measured 1,136 horsepower and 996 foot-pounds of torque. We calculated that it should peak at around two hundred five miles per hour."

"Wow. I've always wanted to drive one of these."

With a smug grin, Nora threw Derek the keys, "Well, what are you waiting for then?"

The main hangar door slowly creaked open to reveal the abandoned airstrip they were on before.

Derek's eyes widened, "Merry Christmas."

CHAPTER TWENTY-ONE

TEST DRIVE

WEDNESDAY, JULY 12, 2028

Derek gripped the wheel of one of his dream cars. He couldn't believe he was actually sitting in a Dodge Viper ACR. The Behemoth team had set a mock track on the airstrip, but first, Derek wanted to see how fast it could go. So he lined up the car at the end of the runway and revved his engine in anticipation.

Deep breath in….

Deep breath out….

Gas in….

Clutch out….

The Viper launched forward with a loud screech and a massive cloud of smoke as the tires failed to find the grip they needed.

"Whoa! Easy girl, easy!" Derek screamed while grasping the wheel with a death grip.

He eased off the gas and regained control. Shifting into second, the Viper came out of its shell, allowing Derek to push it harder. Third and fourth gear disappeared as if they were never there. Going over one hundred eighty miles per hour, Derek was approaching the three-quarter mark of the runway, and the Viper still had a lot left in her.

"Come on! Whatcha got!"

It wasn't long before Derek saw a sign that read in big, bold letters, "STOP!" in the distance.

Just as he saw the sign, Derek also saw his speedometer.

"Two hundred already?! Oh, let's go."

Still in fifth gear, Derek slammed the gas pedal as far as it would go.

"Two, oh, one!" he read out loud.

"Two, oh, two!"

"Two, oh, three!"

"Two, oh, four! Come on baby!"

As Derek passed the enlarged stop sign as the Viper hit two hundred six miles an hour. He immediately engaged the brakes and shifted down to fourth, third, then second, allowing his engine to do all the braking. Derek was running out of runway but wasn't worried because he knew the brakes were also upgraded. The Viper rolled to a smooth stop, leaving the front splitter in line with the edge of the runway.

"Oh girl, we are going to get along just fine!"

Derek pulled up next to Mrs. Barnes, "I hit two oh six on that run, and I'll tell you what, it can go faster!"

"You think its speed is impressive? Try our road course out because it's even crazier in the corners... once you get past the first gear wheelspin of course."

Derek hoped she'd say that because even though any car reaching two hundred miles per hour is impressive, the competitors were surpassing it. He knew that if he was going to win this next race, he'd need to have an edge in the corners.

The course utilized the entire airport. There were a lot of fast corners combined with long straights and technical sections through abandoned hangars which created the perfect test track for Derek to get used to his new car. Spin-

ning his wheels through first, he launched himself down the runway. Coming to the first corner, he applied the brakes and downshifted into second for the sharp left turn. To his surprise, the car started sliding.

"Oh, come on!" Derek yelled in frustration as he counter-steered and straightened out.

After the brief straightaway, Derek saw the next left turn up ahead. This time, he put more faith into the vehicle and put his car into third gear for the slightly faster corner. But, to his astonishment, the car took the corner flat.

"Oh! You're acting like a real racecar. I gotta keep my speed up in the corners so aerodynamics can do its job."

Derk slammed the gas pedal and shifted his way up into fifth. Instead of slowing down for the upcoming right, he sped up and took the turn at over one hundred twenty miles per hour.

"That's more like it!"

After weaving around the back lot cones, Derek crossed the airstrip like a pedestrian and headed towards the empty hangars. It was a straight shot through, but it was narrow. This didn't faze Derek in the slightest. He rushed through those hangars at over a hundred miles per hour as if it were second nature to him. Shifting down into fourth, Derek took his foot off the throttle and coasted to the other side of the runway. The hangars on this side of the track weren't empty. The cones were directing him in between several small airplanes.

"Oh, come on guys! You couldn't remove the Cessnas before setting up the track?"

Slowing down to third gear, Derek weaved through the planes as fast as he could. Even with the tight cornering, the Viper was still managing to stay flat. After leaving the hangars, there was one final loop before restarting the lap. Derek held his ground and kept accelerating. He eased off the throttle and pushed the car as fast as possible through the turn. He could hear the tires screeching, begging him to slow down so they could grip the road. So Derek eased off the gas as the corner progressed, allowing the tires to do their job. Once the turn was over, Derek downshifted into the straight and disappeared into another test lap.

Several hours passed, and Derek had completed numerous test laps. He finally had to call it quits because he ran out of fuel. As he idled back into the main hangar, he parked next to where Nora was sitting, reading her book.

"I take it you don't like it then?" She said sarcastically.

"Yep. I love it to pieces."

"Good. Why don't we head over to my office so you can sign some paperwork so you can actually use it this weekend?"

"Sounds good to me," Derek said with the biggest grin.

Nora spent the next hour or so explaining to Derek all of the legalities of lending him this car for the final race, and Derek signed all of the necessary forms.

"Alright. That's the last of the paperwork for us to go over." Nora exclaimed, "Now you just got to go win that race!"

"Excellent! Thank you so much, Mrs. Barnes!"

"Oh, I nearly forgot to tell you. If you place on the podium for the tournament, you can buy the loaner car from us with the prize money."

Derek stopped and turned around, "Oh really?"

"Mmhmmm," Nora hummed, "she could be yours."

Derek smiled in disbelief, "I might have to take you up on that."

CHAPTER TWENTY-TWO

MOMENT OF TRUTH

SATURDAY, JULY 15, 2028

D erek was admiring the Viper in the shop as Charlie approached.

"She is a beaut' isn't she Stetson?"

"Amen to that!" Derek replied, "Did you get it?"

"Yessir! One race map coming up." Charlie said while throwing up a map onto the workbench.

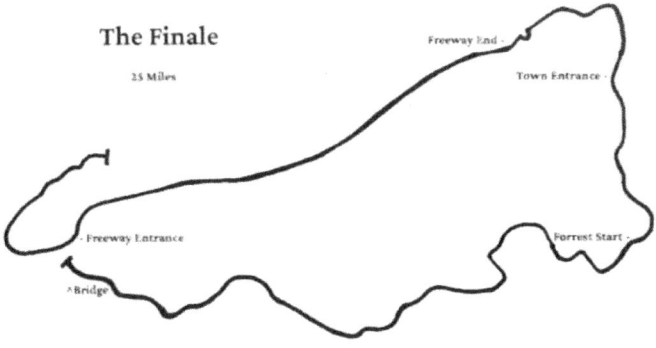

Scratching his head, Charlie explained the course Derek would have to tackle.

"Alright, see here? The beginnin' bit contains a lot of twists and turns until you hit the southern coastline. You'll run parallel with the beach for a bit, then you'll take a fast left chicane onto where the highway starts. Once there, it's my understandin' that you'll be racin' on the entire freeway, so no off-ramps. Where we're goin' to have issues though is the very end of the highway. For the slight left turn at the end, you can probably just lift off the gas a little instead of braking, but you are immediately faced with a dead-stop roundabout. You'll have to go from two hundred-plus miles per hour, down to fifty or so, give or take."

Derek gulped, "Do you think that roundabout will be an issue?"

"Well, this whole course is an issue if you make a wrong move. But yes, I do believe this roundabout will be a big issue. Now, back to what I was gettin' at. After the traffic circle of doom, you'll be navigatin' through some tighter corners but nothing too serious. Once you get to the suburbs though, that's when things will get really interesting. The roads are narrow, which particularly sucks because, with the exception of a couple of hard right turns, it's still a fast-paced section of road."

"Well shit," Derek swore.

Charlie chuckled, "You think that's bad, you're only a little over halfway done! Once you get out of the suburbs, you'll have some technical parts that lead straight toward the forest where you'll be spendin' the rest of the race. The first several miles into the treeline are all very technical corners; a lot of sharp turns and a couple that almost look like hairpins. Fortunately, it does open up for a while right there in the middle, includin' an arrow-straight road right there."

"Well, that's good."

"Don't get your hopes up, after that long stretch of straight follows even more technical turns. Here's the kicker, from this point on, you'll still be flooring it. All of these corners leading to the finish line are deceivin'ly fast; you shouldn't even have to brake for most of them."

"Wait a minute!" Derek interjected, "You mean to tell me those esses require close to no braking?!"

"Like I said, deceivingly fast."

How long is this race in total?" Derek asked.

"Mr. Sullivan said that it was 24 miles long."

"Good times"

"Yep, after the fast esses, you'll have a bridge that's a quarter mile long give or take to push your car as fast as you can. The finish line is on the other side of that bridge."

Derek sighed, "Well, what are we waiting for? Let's get this show on the road!"

Without missing a beat and with a completely straight face, Charlie replied, "The race doesn't start for 'nother two hours; that's what we're waiting for!"

"Drivers! Start! Your! Engines!"

The five cars roared to life. Derek saw Carmen's Miata to his left, Warren's GT, and Sandra's Veneno behind him, and even though he couldn't see him, he knew that Killian's Ferrari was behind them. Everyone was itching to go, and everyone was ready to win. All that was left to do now was wait for the flag to drop.

A race official walked onto the road and lifted two flags above his head. Derek could feel the anticipation in the air. The smell of racing fumes and the sound of controlled explosions in each cylinder had everyone on the edge of their seats.

The flags dropped, and the race began!

In the heat of the moment, Derek forgot the Viper's one flaw. He slammed the gas pedal down and spun the rear tires profusely. Desperately wrestling the car back into control, Derek watched all three of his competitors pass him effortlessly.

"Okay, that start sucked," he told himself, "I miss my four wheel drive right about now."

To nobody's surprise, the cars with all-wheel drive, the Miata and the Veneno, took the early lead, leaving everyone else to play catch up. Fortunately, Derek's Viper effortlessly demolished the corners, allowing him to catch up to Killian. Derek attempted to pass Killian with no success. Instead of trying to overtake him straight up, Derek switched strategies and stayed behind his slipstream. Finally, Killian made a mistake. On the corner leading to the beach, Killian stayed inside the painted lane as if it were a Sunday drive. This opened up the inside for Derek to pass.

"Oh, Killian," Derek muttered, "this is racing boy, not a cruise."

In that same corner, the GT and the Veneno passed Carmen's miata. At the end of the day, they had a much higher top speed than her. Derek was chasing her down. Keeping to his drafting strategy, Derek stayed behind Carmen until the next turn. Derek recognized that after this chicane, it would be the highway segment. He knew that he would have to carry a lot of speed out of the corner if he were to have any chance at keeping up with the leaders. The corner approached, and to Derek's surprise, Carmen hit the brakes. At two hundred miles per hour, Derek released the gas and swerved out of the way. Mid-corner, he slammed on the pedal again and slingshot out of the chicane and onto the highway, where he just saw Warren's GT make the same move past the Veneno.

CHAPTER TWENTY-THREE

WHAT GOES AROUND, COMES AROUND

SATURDAY, JULY 15, 2028

Now in third place, Derek had to put his top speed against his opponents. He continued to draft off Sandra's Veneno and kept his pace climbing. It wasn't long before his speedometer had surpassed the technician's expectations... by a lot. He was going two hundred twenty-five miles per hour drafting the Lamborghini, and he wasn't even at the redline yet on his tachometer!

"Two-oh-five my ass! It's still not enough to pass these guys but at least I can keep up!" Derek exclaimed.

Unfortunately, Derek wasn't the only one drafting off of his opponents. Looking to his left, he saw Killian steadily passing him by. However, Derek wasn't overly concerned. He knew he was not in the fastest car here, and there was a lot of race left to go. The trick is to keep up with the leaders and wait for them to make a mistake.

Looking back in his rearview mirror, Derek noticed that Carmen was at least four car lengths behind him.

"Damn, I guess she never figured out her gearbox. She'll come back in the tail-end."

Bringing his attention back to the main issue, Derek needed a strategy to pass Killian. He knew he'd have to utilize Killian's slipstream, but his head gasket could blow at this speed if he tried to push too hard. Meanwhile, the Veneno passed Warren's GT. Derek knew how much Killian despised Warren for winning last year and hoped he wouldn't do anything irrational. Unfortunately, Derek was wrong. Now drafting off of Warren, Killian gently nudged Warren's rear bumper. At two hundred-plus miles per hour, nothing is gentle. Warren's GT started to swerve, allowing Killian to pass. While Warren wrestled his car for control, Derek could dodge him and regain third place. Unfortunately, Derek's small victory was short-lived because the Ford caught back up to Derek after regaining control almost instantly. Although Derek tried defending his position by making his car as wide as possible, Warren's car had a faster top speed and made short work of Derek's defenses. Even though his Viper was breaking expectations, it wasn't enough to make headway on the highway. Warren used the momentum from Derek's slipstream to slingshot past him and catch up to Killian in one swift motion. Killian didn't realize what happened until he was staring at a set of Ford GT tail lights.

Derek couldn't help but chuckle, "Karma buddy! That's what you call Karma!"

Looking back, he noticed that Carmen's Miata was even farther behind.

"Shit, if she gets any farther behind, she won't make it at all, and we aren't even half way through the highway yet!"

It was at this moment Derek knew what he needed to do. He let off the gas and let the car naturally slow down, allowing Carmen to catch up. Pulling beside her, Derek looked into her cockpit and tapped his wrist, signaling her to draft off him. Carmen shook her head in agreement. Derek hit the gas and pulled in front of her. Carmen was practically touching Derek's rear bumper when he started accelerating again. Instead of leaving her in the dust, Carmen could utilize his slipstream to achieve new top speeds that she hadn't been able to achieve before, just like how Derek did in his Viper moments ago. Because Derek didn't have anyone to draft off of, he couldn't reach two twenty-five like before, but he still wasn't slouching either. He could assist Carmen up to two hundred twelve miles per hour before he could feel the Viper groan at the redline.

They slowly caught up to Killian as he fell behind the leaders. Then, Killian's Ferrari suddenly hit a bump in the road, broke loose, and started swerving wildly. While Killian wrestled his car for control, Derek and Carmen quickly passed him. Killian was visibly furious, and rightfully so; nobody likes being in last place. Carmen and Derek were side-by-side once more. Even though they couldn't speak directly to one another, they knew what to do. They both knew they were in the slowest cars there, and if either wanted to finish on the podium, they would have to work together. Derek and Carmen continued their drafting strategy in an attempt to catch up with the Ford and the Lamborghini.

As Carmen was passing Derek, Killian was attempting to pass Carmen. Unfortunately, the three of them failed to realize that they were about to come to the end of the highway. Just as they went three wide, the road dropped from three lanes into two. Killian forced himself into the middle, removing what little room Derek and Carmen had between themselves and the walls on either side. It was becoming claustrophobic for the three racers. As the three racers thought it couldn't get any worse, they rapidly approached the next left turn. It became a game of chicken. Who had the guts to brake last and take the lead? Derek remembered what Charlie said about this corner. He shouldn't have to brake at all; just ease off the gas! The corner approached, and to nobody's surprise, Killian was the first on his brakes, and Carmen followed shortly after. On the other hand, Derek kept his foot off the brakes entirely and let his car's aerodynamics keep him planted on the road as he made it through the left turn.

Once they made it through, they all discovered trouble at the roundabout. The Lamborghini Veneno tore straight through the traffic circle and went airborne!

Chapter Twenty-Four

Devastation

Saturday, July 15, 2028

Carmen, Derek, and Killian slammed on their brakes as they watched their competitor fly through the air like an airplane. The Lamborghini crashed into the road viciously and swerved off the road. Derek was the first to ease off the brakes and take on the roundabout. When he exited the circle, Derek could see Sandra safely exiting her car under her own power.

"Thank god she's okay," he sighed.

Once confirming she was okay, the race was back in full swing. Derek had to catch back up with Warren because he decided to help Carmen. Derek could still see Killian and Carmen fighting for third in his mirrors.

"Don't bother yourself with that now. Focus!" Derek lectured.

Shifting into fifth, Derek chased down the GT. Fortunately, he noticed that Warren had to lift off the gas to safely complete the turns. Derek utilized this to his advantage. Trusting in the Viper's aerodynamics to keep him planted on the road, Derek slammed the gas pedal to the floor, entering the right turn. When Derek realized his mistake, his rear wheels had already lost grip and started sliding from under him. Derek quickly countersteered and saved the corner but lost momentum against Warren. Carmen and Killian were growing in Derek's mirrors; he had to act fast. Then, Derek was hit with a stroke of luck. Warren had made the same mistake as Derek on the wide turn. Derek and the other racers wasted no time taking advantage of his mistake. By the time Warren had fixed his error, Derek had already taken the lead, followed by Killian and Carmen. All four racers were within an inch of each other as they approached the suburb. It wasn't long before Warren weaved between them all to regain his position in first place, and Killian finally found his groove because he was quick to follow. Derek and Carmen were now side by side and were surrounded by houses. Derek had to slam on the brakes because a trash can was left out on the sidewalk, allowing Carmen to gain third place. It took Derek a second to collect his bearings after the close call, but he was still in a competitive position. He could see Warren and Killian battling for first. To their surprise, Carmen came from their blind spot and passed both of them!

Derek chuckled, "Good on ya."

The neighborhood roads were getting narrower, and finding a window of opportunity to pass his opponents was harder. Suddenly, Warren took the left turn too tight and ran into a fairly deep puddle caused by someone's broken sprinklers. Derek went wide to avoid him and took third. Up ahead, Derek could see Killian trying to get past Carmen. To Killian's dismay, Carmen was just too fast coming out of the corners. Derek slowed down for the sharper right turn as Warren caught back up.

Derek sighed, "Hello again, Warren."

He swerved around the road defensively to keep Warren's GT at bay.

"I can't let you pass me this time man!"

Derek could tell Warren was getting frustrated.

He chuckled, "I guess I'm doing my job then."

They both had to brake hard for a misleadingly sharp right turn; both lost grip and started to oversteer because they didn't realize how intense the corner was. Warren straightened out first and went bumper to bumper with Derek as they sped out of the following left turn. Carmen and Killian's pace had dramatically decreased because Carmen had to play defense to keep Killian away from her victory. Exiting the suburb, there was a stretch of straight road before the sharp right into the forest. Carmen maintained the lead, followed by Killian, while Derek and Warren tied for third. It was still anyone's race, and they still had at least forty percent left. The four racers approached the forest, passing a thirty-five mile per hour speed limit sign, breaking a hundred miles per hour each.

The sharp right was on top of them. Carmen was at a disadvantage on the outside while Killian snuck up the inside. Carmen timed the corner perfectly. On the other hand, Killian hit the brakes late and understeered straight into Carmen's right quarter panel. She did everything she could to save it, but Killian's speed was too much. Instead of making the turn, she spun out and went straight toward the trees. Warren and Derek witnessed the little Miata struggle to regain control as it hit the dirt. Then it happened, after plowing straight through the first several saplings by the side of the road, the car's passenger side wrapped around a large tree. The car was totaled. There are boomerangs straighter than the unibody structure of Carmen's Miata. Derek was in shock as Warren passed him on the inside. Derek was behind Warren through the following esses. Once they came out of the sharp corner, Derek pulled beside Warren. As Warren looked over, Derek pointed ahead to where Killian was, then shook his fist as if to crush something. Warren nodded, and a temporary alliance was formed to ensure the cheater did not take home the victory.

CHAPTER TWENTY-FIVE

ALLIANCE

SATURDAY, JULY 15, 2028

The forest was becoming denser, and the road required more technical knowledge over speed. Knowing he was in the slower car, Derek stayed behind Warren to maintain his momentum while they chased down Killian's Ferrari. Whether Killian purposely or accidentally put Carmen in the ditch was irrelevant to the two of them. They just wanted to see him lose. The trees and bushes became a blur as they rushed by. At the speed they were going, even the dashed lines looked whole. They weaved in and out of the corners, hitting every apex in between. Then, they found him.

It was a commonly known fact that Killian wasn't the best driver, but it was often made up for with his car doing the rest of the work for him. Money can buy speed, but it fails to buy him skill. Warren and Derek were now right behind

Killian, neither able to see a solid window of opportunity to pass since he was sliding everywhere.

"Come on now Killian! Open up," Derek struggled.

Killian slid wide after a sharp left corner, allowing Derek to sneak his Viper through. Warren tried to pull the same maneuver, but Killian swung the other way before he had the chance. Derek could have easily pulled away here and secured his victory, but he needed to ensure Killian finished third. So instead of running away, Derek paced Killian and kept playing defensively.

"Sorry Killian, I won't win if you're in second. Plus, you need to be taught a lesson."

Killian kept swerving to try and pass Derek, but he kept failing due to Derek anticipating every move and making his car as wide as the road. Then, Warren saw his opportunity because Derek was slowing Killian down. He found his window and raced by, leaving Killian in the dust. Derek and Warren were now keeping pace with each other side by side, taking up the entire road.

Derek shook his fist in the air, "Yes! That'll teach him."

The three remaining racers approached the long straightaway. The guard rails were lined with fans with posters with all their names and inspirational messages like, "Put the pedal to the floor!" It was a friendly reminder that everyone was watching, and the pressure was on.

Warren must have decided that he did his part to keep Killian at bay because once they got onto the straight, he dropped a gear and left quickly. Derek quickly snuck behind him to draft off him, leaving the rest of the road open for Killian to make his move.

"Damn, Warren! We still have a lot of race left to go!" Derek shouted.

Warren noticed that Killian was taking advantage of the window that Derek left open and was displeased. He immediately darted to his right, blocking Killian and leaving room for Derek to pass. They were about halfway through the straight when Derek saw Warren's GT nearly stop in its tracks. It was as if it had disappeared in the blink of an eye.

Derek was confused, "Where'd you go?"

Warren just brake-checked Killian! Derek could see the Ferrari jolt out of the way of the Ford's course. As Killian was passing him, Warren swerved to his left and tried to purposely pit-maneuver Killian!

Derek was appalled by the unsportsmanlike behavior of both of his opponents.

"What is this supposed to be a freaking circus? Maybe an automotive wrestling match? What the hell is wrong with you two!" he swore.

He decided to forget whatever alliance he may have had and just focused on winning the race. With about twenty percent of the race left, Derek attempted to pull away from his opponents and headed into the last technical section of the race.

CHAPTER TWENTY-SIX

THE BRIDGE

SATURDAY, JULY 15, 2028

C harlie was right. The last stretch of the race was very fast-paced despite its technicality. Derek was cutting through corners at two hundred miles per hour left and right. The only problem was Killian and Warren. The three racers were bumper to bumper as they weaved through the forest. Who was going to take the victory? Even though Derek had the lead, it was still anyone's race. Warren found an opportunity to get on the inside next to Derek. They were a mere centimeter away from each other at most. Being behind the two again, Killian desperately tried to find an opening. An opening that never came. To combat this, Killian decided to make one. Coming out of a left corner, Killian snuck between the two cars enough to tap on Warren's bumper, momentarily causing him to lose control. Warren furiously shut the door on him.

"Those two are going to make us all crash!" Derek worried.

Derek then decided to take a risky move. He let off the gas and gently slid back toward Killian. Without missing a beat, Killian took advantage of Derek's actions. Now the roles were reversed. Derek was trying to find an opening between his two opponents.

"Oh shit. That went way better in my head," Derek thought, "Now what do I do?"

Even though Derek didn't have much time to figure it out, he was at the advantage of not being involved in the bumper-car match between the leaders. Killian slammed the side of his Ferrari into Warren's Ford. There was an apparent animosity between these two racers, which was ugly.

"Should I back off some more and give them some space? They're worse than my in-laws!" Derek shouted frustratedly.

Warren returned the blow to Killian while Derek was patiently waiting for a disastrous mistake to ensue. Corner after corner, they kept trading paint aggressively; corner after corner, Derek waited patiently. There were a few moments where he could have slipped in between them, but there was still too much race left, and he could lose the position as quickly as he gained it. Then as Derek looked to his right, the bridge on Texas's southern coast appeared. Finally, he could see the finish line! But unfortunately, several sparks landed on his windshield before Derek could revel in the scenery.

"Oh, for Pete's sake guys! Stop sending sparks all over the paint! It's a RENTAL!"

The two leaders couldn't hear him; they wouldn't have listened even if they could. Killian slammed into the Ford again. There were only three more turns left, and Derek had to move fast. Then, without warning, fortune favored the patient. Warren was tired of his opponent slamming into him, so when Killian made another attempt to slam into him, he hit the brakes and dodged. Killian missed the Ford completely and nearly hit a tree. The Ferrari slammed on the brakes as he spun to a halt. There was one more corner left before the final straightaway on the bridge. Because of his maneuver, Warren had lost all of his momenta. While Derek, on the other hand, powered through the corner at full speed! Derek took the lead on the home straight, accelerating hard from over one hundred fifty miles per hour. The race wasn't over, though, for Warren sneaked behind Derek and was drafting him. They had a quarter mile left to go, the camera helicopters hovered right above the finish line, and Warren was trying to pass Derek. Warren regained the upper hand as he gained speed on Derek's Viper. Both cars had breached two hundred miles per hour... but Warren had made his move a fraction of a second too late. Derek Stetson crossed the finish line at the end of the bridge first, making him the winner of the final race in the Behemoth Grand Prix.

CHAPTER TWENTY-SEVEN

RISING TENSIONS

SATURDAY, JULY 15, 2028

Derek and Warren pulled up at the beach directly adjacent to the finish line. After parking and stepping out of their vehicles, Warren walked over to Derek.

"Good race, sir."

Derek looked disgusted, "Was it? What do you call that move where you purposely attempted to spin Killian out after nearly wrecking him with that brake maneuver you did? Because where I come from, that's called dirty racing!"

"Oh come on, man! You saw what he did to Carmen! He's just lucky I missed!"

"Excuse me?" Carmen interjected, "I can defend my own honor, thank you very much."

Warren had a blank expression, "Carmen... Uh, how are you?"

Even with her right arm in a casted sling and her face bruised, Carmen still managed to scare the everloving crap out of the two boys.

"A little banged up," she responded, "I'll be better once that brat shows up so I can pummel him!"

Warren tensed up, "Get in line."

Derek started laughing.

"What are you laughing at, Stetson?!" Warren yelled.

Laughing even harder, Derek replied, "I was debating whether I should break up this upcoming fight of yours, but I'd rather see a crippled Carmen whip both your and Killians' asses when he shows up."

Carmen couldn't help but snicker as well.

"Not to mention...." Derek added, "If y'all get disqualified for fighting, I get the victory by default, and I wouldn't mind the payday."

"Whatever. I'm not scared of you man." Warren rebutted.

This made Derek laugh harder, "Why would you be scared of me? She's the one who'll knock out anyone who'd stand in her way between her and Killian."

Then, who should arrive but Killian in his Ferrari.

"Well, ladies and gentlemen, that is my cue to go grab a seat and some popcorn. I'll see you around."

Derek sat at a nearby bench and waited for the show to start.

Carmen threw the first verbal assault, "Hey dumbass! Ever heard of the term, "right of way?" You damn near killed me!"

"And who do you think you are? Slamming into me like that, I ought to kick your ass!" Warren added.

"You tell 'em you two!" Derek shouted mockingly from the sidelines.

"Woah, woah, woah! Guys!" Killian shouted, "Look, it's just a race!"

Warren threw the first punch without hesitation. Killian fell to the floor.

"How does that feel, prick?"

Killian looked up at Warren, "I'm pretty sure your mother hit you harder than that as a child!"

Warren kicked him in the chest.

"Warren!" Carmen yelled, "That's enough!"

When Warren grabbed him by the collar, Killian struggled to stand, "Give me one reason why I don't beat you within an inch of your life, Briggs!" Warren threatened.

"Easy!" A lady's voice came from behind, "If you put one more finger on him, you would be officially eliminated, and you stand no chance of winning this event. Not to mention my friends on either side of me are police officers ready to take you away."

Warren dropped Killian and turned around, "You know Mrs. Barnes, you're very good at giving advice, you know that?"

Mrs. Barnes wasn't enthused, "Mmhmm, shut up. Last I checked, you swung first. Go set up at the stage, all of you."

They all started walking away.

"That includes you, Stetson!"

Uncrossing his legs, Derek stood up and walked towards Mrs. Barnes, "That was one hell of a show, huh?"

Unamused, Mrs. Barnes replied, "Don't you usually stop these things before they get out of hand?"

"Normally, I try to, but I figured it would be safer for me to watch this round."

"You think they're angry now? Wait until they hear my speech." Nora threatened as she walked away.

On the beach, a temporary stage was set up, surrounded by screaming fans. Nora Barnes took the stage.

"Good evening, everyone; how'd you all like that race, huh?!" The fans roared. "That's what I like to hear! Now, before I move on to announcing the winners of this year's Grand Prix, I have several announcements to make, and I have a strange feeling that they won't be very popular either. As many of you know, the Behemoth Grand Prix was founded to create the most diverse race the nation has ever seen. BUT! We've noticed these past couple of years, this year especially, that supercars have been taking over the starting grid. This is not because we didn't diversify the playing field, no. It's because there wasn't a definite way for us to measure competitiveness amongst our racers. Our current system is very flawed in that regard. We've had numerous complaints from drivers and viewers alike to address this issue. In addition, we are proud to claim that we are an amateur event! I mention this because, over the years, this competition has only been getting faster and more dangerous. This year, we at Behemoth Parts have decided to hit two birds with one stone. From now on, every vehicle entered in the Behemoth Grand Prix must not exceed a power-to-weight ratio of fifteen horsepower per hundred pounds!"

The crowd was going ballistic.

Nora continued, "These new rules are now in place to ensure the safety of our drivers and to encourage diversity in the competition. Thank you."

Mrs. Barnes remained quiet to let the crowd let out their frustrations.

"I am sorry for the disappointing news, but changes had to be made to keep everyone safe. Now... who wants to hear the results of this year's Behemoth Grand Prix!?"

The crowd's boo's turned into cheers of joy on the flip of a dime.

CHAPTER TWENTY-EIGHT

RESULTS AND REWARDS

SATURDAY, JULY 15, 2028

"Can the top five racers come up to the stage please?" Mrs. Barnes announced.

As the racers entered, the crowd thundered with applause. Every racer was waving to their fans.

"Alright!" Mrs. Barnes interrupted, "That's what I'm talking about! Do you want to know who won!?"

The crowd went even crazier. Then, when Nora waived her hand, they settled down.

"In fifth place... with thirty-seven points... Ms. Sandra Dorette in her 2013 Lamborghini Veneno!"

Everyone applauded while Sandra stepped forward to shake Mrs. Barnes's hand.

Nora conversed with Sandra off-mic, "How are you holding up, dear?"

"Oh, I'm okay. I'm bummed I didn't get a chance to finish this race, but I'm happy I made it this far," Sandra replied.

"Well, I'm sure glad we got to witness you race again. I'm gonna miss you."

They hugged briefly, and Sandra walked to the back of the stage.

"We had a really close race this year folks! Second through fourth place were all separated by *ONE POINT EACH*!" Nora waited for the crowd to settle, "Now. In fourth place... with forty-three points... Mr. Warren Stonewood in his 2016 Ford GT!"

To Warren's surprise, the crowd's response was mixed, and Mrs. Barnes was about to explain why.

"Mr. Stonewood, I would like to congratulate you for coming this far. But I will have you know if it were solely up to me, I would've kicked you out before you could open your mouth to object. You blatantly ignored Behemoth rules and procedures with that pit maneuver attempt. Alas, you didn't qualify, so consider yourself lucky we let you claim a place, period."

Warren was speechless, and his face went pale. He shook her hand cautiously and left backstage.

Nora put her smile back on as if nothing had happened, "Who's ready for the Top Three!?"

After the dramatic pause, Mrs. Barnes continued, "Alrighty then. In third place... for ten-thousand dollars... with forty-*four* points... Ms. Carmen Winters in her 1994 Mazda Mx-5 Miata!"

The crowd exploded with joy. They loved seeing an import take on and defeat numerous supercars.

Carmen approached Mrs. Barnes, "Thank you for this opportunity Mrs. Barnes!"

"Oh please dear, thank you for giving us one hell of a show! Not to mention you can come back next year and show that prick over there who's the boss," Nora winked.

Carmen chuckled lightly, "Oh you can count on it Ma'am."

Carmen raised her fist in the air and ignited the crowd again.

"Alright, folks! Only two left! Now. In second place... for one hundred thousand dollars... with forty-*five* points... Mr. Killian Briggs in his 2018 Ferrari FXX-K EVO!"

The crowd applauded more for Killian than for Warren, but not by much.

"Mr. Briggs, how nice to see you again as the runner up." Nora insulted.

Killian sighed, "Just another year of trying."

Nora wasn't amused, "Look, son, you're flirting with disqualification, ya' hear? I understand *most* of your faults were accidental, but you're pushing your luck. I'd hate to see a young man like yourself get disqualified after the amount of work you've put toward this competition."

Killian sighed disappointedly, "I promise I'll be better next year."

"Good, now smile for the fans! They can't wait to see you next year!"

Killian smiled and waved as he headed back.

"Okay, now folks. You already know who it is!" Nora shouted, trying to talk over the screaming fans, "In first place, for one million dollars, with forty-eight points, Mr.

Derek Stetson in his 1969 Dodge Charger Daytona and his 2016 Dodge Viper ACR!"

The crowd was louder than a V8 when Derek started walking forward to receive his oversized check.

"Congratulations Mr. Stetson! Talk about an underdog story."

Derek wiped away his tears of joy, "I don't even know what to say."

Mrs. Barnes smiled, "Well, you want that Viper you just drove?"

"Oh jeez. God yes! Like this day couldn't get any better!" Derek said, shaking her hand. "May I say something to the crowd?"

Nora nodded, "Of course."

Derek took the microphone, "I just wanted to thank my beautiful wife and daughter back home for pushing me to overcome my fears and supporting me through this whole event and express my sorrows for Michael's family... I didn't know him well, but he was still an invaluable part of our team." Derek took a moment to collect himself, "Well, I can only assume my family is watching on the television right now, so... Girls! I LOVE YOU SO MUCH! WE WON!"

The crowd could have shattered glass with their cheers.

The next day, Derek was cleaning out his belongings from his assigned garage with the other racers when Mrs. Barnes showed up and called the podium finishers to the common area.

"Congratulations, you three. You earned it. As Killian is well aware, I'm here to officially reserve your spot for next year's event, provided you want to." Then she turned to Killian, "Can I assume you want to participate next year?"

Killian replied with a simple, "Yes ma'am."

"Good," she turned toward Carmen, "and you dear?"

Carmen glared at Killian, "Oh hell yes."

Then she turned toward Derek, "How about you Derek?"

Derek paused to think, "Mrs. Barnes, I thank you from the bottom of my heart for this opportunity, but I cannot race next year."

Carmen and Killian turned toward him in shock.

Mrs. Barnes reacted the same way, "Really? I think we can all agree that you are one of the most skilled drivers here!"

The other two nodded their heads in agreement.

"Sorry guys. This tournament put a lot of stress on my family and I can't put them through that again. I got what I came here for, now it's time to go home."

Everyone was silent.

Nora cleared her throat, "Well, I'm sad to see you go. It was a pleasure watching you race this year Mr. Stetson."

Carmen walked over and gave Derek a hug, "Thanks for looking out for me man. It was awesome racing with you."

Killian slowly walked towards Derek, too, "Uhm, thanks for everything man. It's nice to know that I'm not alone."

Derek swept away tears, "You ain't alone kid. You got talent. You just gotta harness it a little better is all."

"Thank you sir. It was nice racing with you."

Derek called him in for a hug as well.

Wiping away tears again, Derek said his final goodbyes, "I'm going to miss racing with y'all!"

CHAPTER TWENTY-NINE

REMINISCENCE

SUNDAY, JULY 16, 2028

It was time for Derek to drive himself home. Cruising was one of Derek's favorite things to do because there wasn't anything to worry about. You could just turn your brain off and listen to your engine purr, the tires against the pavement, or listen to relaxing music if the situation calls for it. You can have the windows down, feel the wind hit your face, admire the scenery, and feel the motor's vibration shake your worries away like it's sifting for gold. Derek could spend all day on the road if you'd let him. He felt his car was a home away from home where nothing else mattered.

He thought about his adventure from the past several weeks. Chuckling about some of the outrageous cars that showed up, like the Ford Raptor. Remembering the adrenaline from chasing down top-of-the-line supercars in his ancient Dodge. Recollecting the look on everyone's face when they realized that someone had given him the wrong tires and how often he had to pull Carmen off of Killian before she tore him to pieces. How mentally scarred Killian is and how he has no one there to help him cope with life, and how Carmen has to provide for herself and her son on her own.

Derek took a moment of silence for his crewmate Michael who had passed away helping him race.

"I did it buddy. We won." Derek cried.

Derek's phone broke the silence. Quickly wiping away tears, Derek answered, "Hello?"

"Mr. Stetson?"

"Yes?"

"Hey! It's Nora."

"Oh hey Mrs. Barnes! You miss me already?"

She laughed, "You know it! I just wanted to give you a quick update."

Derek paused, "An update? On what?"

"The Behemoth team was sad to see you go, and we respect your decision. However, we would like to offer you a position here at Behemoth as a consulting mechanic and racer."

Derek's eyes lit up, "What does that entail?"

"During the off-season, you'd be our on-call mechanic who'd give us advice if we needed it. We'd also call you regarding advice on racing matters such as car selection."

"Oh wow. That sounds amazing!"

"Just you wait Mr. Stetson, it gets better! During the season, you become an assistant mechanic and crew chief to other racers."

"Like Charlie!?"

"Yes sir! Exactly."

"That's an amazing offer ma'am. How much are you offering though?" Derek asked hesitantly.

Mrs. Barnes laughed, "Name your price."

Derek's jaw dropped to the floor.

After talking logistics for an hour or so, Mrs. Barnes hung up the phone, and Derek continued his journey home. Initially, Derek was still concerned about his financial situation because one payday is not a fix-all solution; over the years, it will deplete if there's no source of income, especially after paying off all of their debt and the house. But now, Derek can breathe easier because there's a steady income, his family can revel in the fruits of his labor, and now Derek can enjoy his family to the fullest every day.

CHAPTER THIRTY

THERE'S NO PLACE LIKE HOME

SUNDAY, JULY 16, 2028

T he sun was setting on the Stetson homestead when Derek arrived. He revved his engine several times before shutting her off to alert his family that he was home safe. Autumn knew the sound well. She slammed the door open and bolted across the lawn to her dad's car. Derek's seatbelt hadn't even finished retracting when she opened the car door and launched herself into her dad's arms.

"Oof!" Derek exclaimed, "I missed you too, my Autumn leaf." She squeezed tighter, "I guess you couldn't wait for me to get to the living room carpet huh?"

Autumn shook her head no in his chest. Derek looked outside to see his beautiful wife laughing and recording the whole thing on her phone. Despite Autumn's snake-like hugs, Derek managed to get out of the car and walk toward

Shannon. With Autumn still attached, Derek gave his wife a hug.

"AUTUMN SANDWICH!" Her parents yelled collectively.

"Ah! No!" Autumn squirmed until she gained her freedom. Derek and Shannon chuckled as she ran away.

"What a goof," Shannon tried saying with a straight face.

"Yep, that's our daughter."

Derek locked his car door and walked with Shannon inside.

Autumn was full of questions and wonderment.

"How many cars were there?! How fast were you going?! Did you keep the new car? Why did your old car blow up!? Did anyone else's car blow up?! Did you see that one car go flying?!"

"Woah easy there!" Derek interrupted, "One question at a time!"

Autumn put her hand on her chin and stared at the ceiling in deep thought as if she were only allowed to ask one question, "Did you make any friends, daddy?"

Derek smiled; that wasn't a question he was expecting, "Yes, dear, I made some friends while I was away."

"How many? What were their names?"

"Autumn! One at a time silly." Derek laughed, "Let's see... There's Mrs. Barnes, the race organizer. She was really nice. And Mr. Sullivan, the racer coordinator. He was super cool.

There's Carmen obviously. We helped each other out a couple times at the races. I think Killian might be my friend, but he and I didn't always get along."

"Oooooh," Autumn exclaimed, "What was the coolest car you saw there?"

"Hmmm, that's a tough one. There were so many! I didn't even know the name of some of them. If I had to choose one, it would have to be my Viper. I really like that car."

"Oo! Did you keep the car? Did you keep the car?!"

"Yes my Autumn-leaf, I got to keep the car."

"Really?" Shannon interrupted.

"Yep, since my Daytona was totaled, I traded it in for the Viper. The difference was taken out of my winnings."

Shannon nodded in surprised approval.

"How about the racetracks daddy?! What was your favorite? Mine was the jungle one where you won!"

"Oh ya, that was really fun. There were a lot of super fast parts that I really liked."

"Okay you two," Shannon interrupted, "We gotta get to bed. You can ask your daddy all the questions you want tomorrow morning at breakfast."

"Fiine!" Autumn groaned.

Autumn was allowed to camp out in her parent's room that night as a special treat. She snuggled between them and made herself comfortable, often at her parent's expense. Finally, after they are all bundled together under the covers, they said their goodnights:

"Goodnight, my love," said Shannon lovingly.

"Goodnight my love," returned Derek

"Goodnight weirdos!" Groaned Autumn.

After they finished laughing, Derek and Shannon shared a kiss and went to bed.

"There will be days where I miss racing. I'll miss feeling all the power from the engine vibrate through my soul and how the car would force me deeper into my seat when I downshift. The whole world would pass me in a blur as all my problems, fears, and sorrows drifted away. But now that I have redeemed myself, and brought prosperity to my family, I can safely say that I will never long for it ever again."

Epilogue

After her long flight from Texas, Carmen was finally home in Tucson, Arizona.

"Honey! I'm home!" She yelled across the house.

"Hey mom!" Cole Winters, her son, replied as he walked out of the kitchen, "Holy shit! Are you okay?!"

He rushed to his mom's aid. "I knew you got into an accident, but they didn't show how bad it was on the air!" Cole said while sporadically looking for an ice pack.

"Cole!"

He stopped where he stood.

"Calm down. I'm fine. The paramedics gave me a clean bill of health. Just a broken arm and a bunch of bruises!"

"Oh, okay." Cole calmly sat down next to her on the couch. "I take it third place isn't enough for my college tuition huh?"

Carmen sighed, "For a semester or two maybe, but we'd still need a loan for the rest of it. The one downside of wanting to go to the big schools, honey."

"I could go to a community college?"

"Is that what you want?"

"Not really, but...."

"Then you aren't going. I can win this race honey. I should've won this time if it weren't for that jerk!"

Cole looked at his mom with concern, "The guy in the Ferrari right?"

"Ugh, Killian."

"Can you save the Miata for next year?"

"No, it was totaled. But Behemoth gave me an additional five grand for it since there were still a lot of usable parts in it, so that's nice."

"What are you going to do?" Cole asked.

"Well, I got fifteen grand from this past race. Considering the new rule changes for next year, that should be more than enough to build something competitive."

"That sounds fair. What if that Killian guy gets in the way again?"

"Don't worry Cole. I'm going to get my revenge on that jerk next year."

Acknowledgements

I would like to thank my family and friends who directly helped me write and proofread this book. Their help was instrumental to its completion.

- Mom

- Kristen

- Claire

- Grandma Lynette

- Grandpa Rusty

- Uncle Andrew

I would also like to thank my Launch team for helping me get this book off the ground

- Aaliyah

- Aaron

- Augustin

- The AutoZone Crew

- Billy

- Uncle Brandon

- Dad

- The Clement Family

- Erwin

- Jacob

- Kieran

- The Rauls Family